Marked for Adventure

by JSD Johnston

Marked for Adventure

Tomo 1, parsa i

of Peyton Drake's Omni Tale

by JSD Johnston

INTERACTIVE CONTENT

Each chapter has at least one underlined interactive link to related content

A MASTER LINK LIST TO THE EMBEDDED CONTENT IS LOCATED AT THE END OF THIS BOOK AFTER THE GLOSSARY

Questions? Contact Genie@OmniOcademy.com

About this Omni Tale

The **Tactile version comes with links and twixt-page inserts, as well a key to unlock bonus text** ranging from a paragraph to an entire scene. Story options include **Tangible Gift Kits, Advent{ure} Calendar**, our popular **Teachizz™ Edition** (available as a printable 8.5x11 PDF with links & wide margins for lesson-leader notes), and a full curriculum of **Omnimmersive Learning Experiences** lessons.

Plus, each 7-novella arc comes with its own extras such as a **100-day action journal, coloring & doodling book, online escape-room-style game, trading cards, Bells & Whistles book club packet**, and more via OmniTales.com.

ISBN: 978-1-959822-00-4

Published by E. Gads Hill Press

KRAKEN INK

"LIFE IS EITHER A DARING ADVENTURE OR NOTHING." —HELEN KELLER

Reader advisory: Rest assured, the recent earthquakes, tornadoes, hurricanes, fires, and similar forces majeures are unrelated coincidences and have nothing to do with this book. It's not as if there's someone controlling the weather. Experts have a difficult enough time forecasting it! So please just sit back and enjoy your time reading. Nature will sort itself out—one way or the other.

THE MATTER

CHAPTER ONE – THE RED X 1

CHAPTER TWO – WATCHING LIKE A HAWK 9

CHAPTER THREE – THE DUBIOUS DINER 19

CHAPTER FOUR – A CUSTODIAN'S WORK IS NEVER DONE 25

CHAPTER FIVE – THE OCADEMY 34

CHAPTER SIX – FISHING 39

CHAPTER SEVEN – CRISIS AVERTED 47

CHAPTER EIGHT – A GIFT 55

CHAPTER NINE – SEEKING APPROVAL 67

CHAPTER TEN – DOUBLE CHOCOLATE INJUSTICE 73

CHAPTER ELEVEN – WITHOUT A NET 78

CHAPTER TWELVE – POT ROAST & PAPER CLIPS 85

CHAPTER THIRTEEN – AWAITING THE DAWN 94

NOMINALLY ENTERTAINING GLOSSARY 101

ACKNOWLEDGMENTS 118

"Never heard of him, sorry."

"He's in my math class ... I think ... maybe."

"Isn't he that guy from that old rock band?"

"Who?"

CHAPTER ONE – THE RED X

{Kapta An}

Pete Drake was as memorable as parsley garnish.

That was just the way his father liked it. Lt. Drake had gone to great lengths to ensure his son didn't stand out or excel in any way. He treated Pete's potential like it was poison oak—discouraging Pete's dreams and poo-poohing his inventions. When Pete created a secret best-friends-for-life handshake with a classmate, the lieutenant uprooted the family and moved them three time zones away.

The friction-shy fourteen-year-old considered all the fuss unnecessary. It wasn't as though he resisted being ordinary—just the opposite. He'd spent years cultivating a bland façade and hiding his talents. The tactic enabled him to float through life unnoticed and without incident, rarely attracting the attention of the bullies at school. More important, it helped keep the peace at home. He had no reason to think today would be any different—no reason yet.

The sky cracked open with a roar of thunder that was more akin to an anguished scream than an atmospheric boom. As if a switch on the sun had been flipped off, the bright morning instantly turned charcoal grey. Sheets of rain poured off the house's eaves, obscuring the view of anything but water. The neighborhood birds left off mid-chirp, and a noise like the turning of a giant metal gear groaned. All at once, the entire house jolted.

Before Pete could register what was happening, the pelting of agitated water beads ceased. His half-open bedroom window rattled as a luminous sunbeam pierced the glass to cast a rainbow on the opposing Navajo White wall.

"Omnigram for Drake," called a delivery boy on the sidewalk, raising his voice above the shrill squawking of the ferruginous hawk perched in the tree outside Pete's window.

Pete scrambled out of the blanket fort he'd constructed on the floor of his room, taking care not to disrupt the military diorama he'd set up. The delivery of any sort of *gram* was a big occasion at the Drake home. The last messengered communiqué the family received had been a risqué strip-o-gram that arrived at the wrong address—as his father avowed more than once.

Cassie, Pete's mother, answered the courier from her regular spot on the front porch swing. "That's us! Thank you. I … Where'd he go?"

The rainbow faded. The rain-streaked glass rattled again. Pete reached the window only to find the street empty—the messenger and the morning's excitement already dissolved into the grey. Cassie pressed a thumb to her temple and looked far off at nothing, as had become commonplace in recent years.

As Pete turned away, he did a double take at the hawk that now sat on a branch substantially nearer the window, staring straight at him.

That bird gives me the creeps. It's always looking at me like ... Hawks don't eat people, do they?

He shuddered and returned to the center of his room to hunker down inside his threadbare shelter. As he untied the keep's privacy flap, his gaze caught on the only adornment that remained in his room, a marked-up calendar blazoned with a definitive red X. There was no getting around it. It was moving day—again.

The sight of the red X always tied Pete in knots. He instinctively grabbed his side to massage his disconcerted pancreas. Despite being unsure what a pancreas did or where it was located, he remained confident in his diagnosis that the organ was ill at ease.

The bulk of his boxes already packed, he reasoned he'd earned a respite and some time alone—alone aside from the two armies assembled in the blanket fort. With greater care than usual he arranged the little green soldiers passed down to him from his father. Their impending battle was to be the last waged at the current coordinates. As such, he intended to make it one for the annals.

He'd outdone himself with the latest addition to his arsenal of custom-built war machinery—a sophisticated, self-arming and repeating catapult. His boyhood collection of marbles sat lined up beside it, positioned at just the right angle for automatic loading and firing. Surveying his well-ordered combat zone and innovative armaments, he pulled his crossed legs in tighter. "Peace at last … Let the carnage begin."

As he picked up a box of matches to ignite a fuse, the steady beat of boots parading through the hall stamped to an emphatic halt. Based on Pete's experience, the silhouetted figure looming in the doorway would brook no procrastination. He held his breath, as if doing so would help him to go unobserved.

Maybe if I just stay quiet and ignore him, he'll eventually just go away.

"Junior, for cryin' out loud," his father scolded. "I already asked you to pack up your room and the head. You're not going to make me ask again, are you?"

"No, sir," Pete muttered, emerging from the security of his quilted war bunker.

"Shoulders back … and no sulking. You know this move is for your own good, son."

So you keep telling me.

Pete's attempt to stand at attention while shaking off the battlefield barbwire that had attached itself to his sock resulted in his nearly knocking over the fort.

"Just what have you got going on in there?" His father stomped over to the fort and pulled back one of its blankets, exposing the upright broom that served as the structure's primary support. "I've been looking for that broom all morning, Junior!"

"Sorry, Dad."

Lt. Drake grabbed the broom handle and yanked. Pete gawped as his field headquarters collapsed into a pile of laundry and the rows of artillery scattered across the linoleum floor. When the sound of rolling marbles ceased, the lieutenant tramped across the heap of mismatched covers and shoved the broom into Pete's hands. "Looks like you'll be needing this after all."

And just like that, before Pete could wipe out so much as a single squadron, his war was preempted. A lump rose in his throat as he examined the remnants of what should have been his greatest victory, and he imagined he heard the strains of a requiem swelling beneath the mound of blankets.

"Now, are you going to pack this mess up, Junior? Or do I have to do it for you?"

Pete quailed at the thought of his newly constructed catapult's fate should his father make good on his threat to pack up the fort. He dropped down on his hands and knees to initiate the hunt for strewn marbles, counting in his head how many he collected and how many he had yet to find.

The uncommonly kempt lieutenant busied himself by consulting his coaster-sized wristwatch and activating a variety of its functions, each of which emitted its own distinct cheep and caused Pete to lose count of his marbles. "The moving men will be here at fourteen-hundred hours, Junior. That gives us just under forty-five minutes."

Thirty-seven marbles down. Sixty-eight to go.

"Where's the packing chart I gave you?"

Forty-one down. Sixty-four to go.

Without waiting for an answer, the lieutenant rummaged through the few remaining papers on his son's desk, wrinkling the detailed design of the latest creation Pete intended to build—someday.

Careful, Dad!

Pete knew better than to say the words aloud, lest he send the lieutenant into yet another harangue about the younger generation's lack of respect. Instead, he stayed silent, imagining his father dressed in a Little Bo Peep getup and combat boots. Picturing his father looking ridiculous always made tongue-biting easier, not to mention far more entertaining.

Thirty-five down ... or did I already do the thirties ... Dang it!

The lieutenant viewed Pete's drawing from several angles, ultimately crumpling it into rubbish.

Pete bit down on the inside of his lip at seeing weeks of work so insouciantly dismissed. His mind flashed to the family's recent nature walk where he witnessed a painstakingly crafted anthill get blithely leveled by a recreational hiker going off trail, walking stick in one hand, coffee mug in the other.

That's exactly how he treats me—like an ant. I will never step on an anthill again.

His father shook the ill-fated sketch in his fist as a warning. "How many times have I told you to drop this inventor nonsense? No good will ever come of it, Junior. I raised you to follow orders, not waste time on useless widgets! If you buckle down and continue on the path your mother and I have outlined for you, you'll be a shoo-in at the Naval Academy and follow in your old man's footsteps. How would you like that?"

Pete forced a wan smile as he considered his father's footsteps, or rather, his footwear. Certainly, the military man's shoes were paragons of proper care, being put to bed each night after a systematic polish once the shoe trees had been locked into place. The slide show in Pete's head clicked forward, and Pete pictured his father in ballet pointe shoes, their pink satin ribbons tied daintily around the lieutenant's hairy calves.

"Now get to work. That's an order!" Lt. Drake lobbed Pete's drawing in the trash, turned about-face, and marched from the room in four-four time.

Get to work?! Every time I work on something, you just wreck it or throw it in the trash!

Pete collected the last of the errant marbles and deposited them in the fabric bag his mother had sewn for the purpose. With a peevish huff, he folded his raggedy fort blankets and placed them in the box marked Old Linens, moving at a pace a tortoise would mock. He was in no hurry to face the inevitable. In an attempt to drown out both the silence and his depressing thoughts, he turned on the television.

"... Another spate of unexplainable wildfires has broken out across the Coastal Plain, and while crews race to put out the flames, a water main has ruptured, caused by the latest in a series of earthquakes. That's the fourth one this week, isn't it, Stu? I can't keep track."

With quiet solemnity, Pete scooped up the army men and let them fall atop the cushy blankets. "You'll be safe in here for now. I have no idea what the terrain will be like at the new place."

"Me neither."

He zeroed in on the television.

Did the TV guy just answer me?

"Gina, seismologists are still scratching their heads over the recent quakes, stating there's no scientific reason they should be occurring and no pattern as to their locations."

> **"On a brighter note, the eleven-year-old boy who'd gone missing last week has been found and is home safe with his family. Randy Floyd was unable to describe where he'd been taken or by whom, but said his captors 'were friendly' and that they let him jump on a cloud. Police have no leads at this time and …"**

The lieutenant stormed back in, glowering as his eyes scoured the room, his fists on his hips.

Pete picked at his thumbnail cuticle, weighing the potential ramifications of addressing his father. "… Looking for something, Dad?"

"For the damn clicker, of course!" He grunted as he upended Pete's boxes in his single-minded quest for the television remote control. "You should be packing, not watching that damn drama box!"

A crisp cracking noise from inside one of the overturned cartons echoed through the spartan room, followed by an indistinct crumbling.

Pete winced, then quietly crossed the room to turn the television off manually. "I packed it, sir."

"Oh … You're damn right you packed it. That's what I told you to do, isn't it?"

No, actually.

"Now where are those damn moving men? I'm docking their pay if they're late!" Once again, the lieutenant was on the march.

Cassie sashayed into the room past her exiting husband, fanning herself with a wax-sealed parchment and inhaling its spiced-fruit fragrance. "Look who received a messengered letter," she cooed in a cheery singsong. She faced the calligraphic lettering toward Pete, running her forefinger under his name in game-show-hostess fashion, then turned the parchment around to display its wax insignia and tassel closure.

“Whoa! I’ve never seen a letter like that before!” He reached toward her outstretched hand in reverence, paying no attention to the rhythmic footfalls approaching.

“Cassie, where did you pack my—” The lieutenant broke off speaking and snatched the correspondence from his wife’s hand before Pete could touch it. His voice dropped to a controlled growl. His nostrils flared. “Where did you get this?”

“A courier just delivered it for P.J. Isn’t it exciting, Peter?” Cassie squinted, her eyes struggling to focus. “I’m sure I’ve seen that seal somewhere before. Do you recognize it, hon?”

The lieutenant turned away, pulled the Swiss Army knife from his pocket, and sliced open the seal. As soon as he glanced at the letter’s contents, he stumbled.

Cassie barely managed to catch him. “Get a chair, P.J., quick!”

Pete dove for his desk chair.

The old wooden seat groaned as the lieutenant collapsed into it, his world collapsing with him.

CHAPTER TWO – WATCHING LIKE A HAWK

{Kapta Be}

"Peter, can you hear me, Peter?" Cassie called, kneeling next to her husband.

Lt. Drake jumped out of the chair and away from her, regarding her as if she were a wraith.

"Peter, what's going on?! Is everything all right?"

He re-tucked his shirt into his pressed trousers and cleared his throat, his composure restored. "It *will* be all right, once we get out of this God-forsaken town!"

That's what you said about the last town, and the town before!

The lieutenant strode across the hall into the bathroom, mumbling as he wadded Pete's letter into a tight ball.

"What is it, hon?" Cassie called, pressing the heels of her palms against her eyes.

"Nothing important, that's for damn sure. Just a sales pitch … misaddressed … wrong house … happens all the time."

"Then shouldn't we deliver it to the correct addressee, hon?"

"Too late now." He flushed the wadded parchment, peering over the toilet bowl to ensure the correspondence was good and gone. "It was meant for me, actually."

Pete debated pointing out that his father's answer made no sense, but decided instead to envision the lieutenant doing the hula in a grass skirt and coconut bra.

Cassie rubbed her temples. "Pity. I was hoping it meant some sort of good news for P.J. And the seal really did look familiar."

"Nothing for you to trouble yourself over, cupcake. Now, go on and take your medication."

"That time already? Where did the morning go?" She pulled a small pillbox from her pocket, popped a tablet into her mouth, tipped her head back, and swallowed hard, her years of practice obviating the need for water.

Pete looked away. The sight of his mother dosing was a grim ritual. The pills always left her slightly groggy, slightly simple, and entirely docile. Nevertheless, it was better than the seizures his mother had suffered after a turbulent quarrel with the lieutenant half a decade ago. The friction that had erupted that night still simmered just below the surface of an opiated truce.

Pete's gaze bypassed his parents to the pool of water collecting on the bathroom floor.

"Dad?"

"The answer is no!"

"Huh? I was just gonna tell you the toilet's overflowing."

"It's that damn letter," the lieutenant snarled, stomping back into the bathroom.

With the bluster of an undefeated medieval knight, he cast a bath towel on the floor and unsheathed a plunger from its decorative encasement, prepared to do battle with the sewer system.

Pete hung back to observe the proceedings from the safety of his room.

"Good thing P.J. didn't pack up the bathroom yet, eh, hon?" Cassie remarked.

The lieutenant braced a boot against the commode, sputtering every expletive he'd learned since joining the Marines.

With his father engrossed in the plumbing debacle, Pete inched over to the trashcan to retrieve the design his father had chucked.

"Don't even think about it," the lieutenant grunted.

Is he talking to me or the toilet?

The can-do patriarch gave two last vigorous plunges, smirking in triumph as the conquered water gurgled and retreated down the commode. He then snapped his fingers and pointed to the floor. "That's for trying to sneak that paper out of the trash."

Question answered.

Pete moaned inwardly and dropped to the ground to complete the obligatory ten push-ups.

You'd think my muscles would be bigger by now.

The lieutenant stepped over Pete's prone form, carting off the waste bin and Pete's drawing with it. "And five more for that look on your face."

Pete's negligible biceps quivered as he pictured his father decked out like Carmen Miranda wielding a pair of maracas and a bongo drum in lieu of a plunger and a dustbin.

While Pete did corporal penance, Cassie picked up the wet towel off the bathroom floor, wrung it out over the tub, and hung it to dry. She then fetched an empty tote bag from under the sink and stuffed her sons' toiletries into it. "I'll carry these for you and Billy. Don't want your toothbrush buried in some box."

"Thanks, Mom."

Her expression stoic, she surveyed Pete's barren bedroom, again massaging her temples. "Anything else I can do to help you finish?"

"Nah, that's okay. I'm pretty much done."

She set the bag down and perched on the edge of the stripped bed. "Come sit by me, P.J."

Pete parked himself on the thin mattress, pouting in skepticism. "So what's Dad's excuse for moving us this time? If it's because of Stacey Larkspur, I swear, it's just a harmless crush. She doesn't even know I exist! And it's not my fault I got an A on my science test. I didn't even study!"

"Calm down, P.J. This move has nothing to do with you. Your father got a promotion is all. That said, you know everything he does is for the good of this family." She cocked her head and glanced down at the spiral pattern her finger was lazily drawing on her thigh—something she tended to do when lost in thought.

One of these days I should ask her to draw that symbol on paper.

"You know, P.J., you may very well be in for a grand adventure at the new place. Who knows what wonders await just around the corner."

"*Pfpfpft*. You say that every time. And it's not just around the corner. It's on another coast!"

She gently brushed the hair off his forehead. "Being the son of a serviceman can't be easy, I imagine. All the relocating, the new schools, starting over again just when you've settled in."

"No wonder they call us Army brats. This lifestyle turns you into a brat!"

"Your father's in the Marines, not the Army."

"You know what I mean. I hate all the moving."

Cassie gazed out the window, a melancholy smile resting on her face, aging her for an instant. "I know how you feel. It's so hard to leave your school friends."

"Friends? What friends?! I don't have any friends here. I haven't had any real friends in years. Dad never lets me."

"What about Billy?"

"Little brothers don't count. Besides, I wouldn't call us *friends* at this point. He's pretty much turned into a bully. He gets more obnoxious with every birthday."

"Well, I'm sure he'll straighten up soon enough. Your father will see to it."

But Dad's a bully too.

The sunlight streaming through his window turned to shadow as the moving truck rolled up to the house like a death cart hired to deliver Pete to the gallows.

"They're here," Pete said flatly, picking at the raw skin around his thumbnail until dots of blood seeped through.

"Finally!" the lieutenant blared from his lookout in the living room, double-timing it out to the front walkway to disseminate orders to the moving crew.

Cassie got up and kissed Pete's forehead. "Don't lose hope, P.J. As one of my closest school friends used to say, 'Where there's hope, there's magic.' I'll see you outside." She slid the tote bag handle over her wrist, rescued the towel from the bathroom, and exited the house, bringing to a close yet another short chapter in her life as a military wife.

Pete stood to regard his soldiers one last time before taping their box shut and trapping them inside. Giving his room the traditional farewell scan, he worked to conjure memories of the place he could one day look back on with a nostalgic smile.

None came.

The familiar shrill of his father's whistle bade the family to line up, close ranks, and stand at attention.

Pete picked up his backpack and slogged toward the front door. His chunky younger brother slammed past him down the narrow hallway, knocking Pete's backpack from his shoulder.

Watch it, Billy ... Bully!

His mother and brother were already in position before Pete made it out to the front yard. Cassie stood posed like a political candidate's wife. Billy puffed out his chest, his chin up and attitude smug.

"On the double, Junior! You'll make us late," his father barked.

But the movers got here early!

"Yes, sir," he murmured, quickening his pace and taking his place in line.

The movers took their time climbing out of the truck. Pete couldn't help but stare at one of the men's unusual arm. The skin was tri-colored. His upper arm was obsidian, while his forearm was the color of pale sand. The limb was a mismatch of freckles and hair, shorter than its counterpart, terminating in a hand of smooth, red-clay skin.

"What's wrong with his arm?" Billy blurted out.

"Billy. It's not nice to say things like that!" Cassie whispered curtly.

The man put his incongruous arm behind his back. "Skin pigment anomaly."

Disregarding the conversation, the lieutenant paced before his family like a general commanding his troops. "By my calculations, we will arrive at the new barracks in ninety-six and a half hours. If the men take turns at the wheel, they should arrive a good four hours ahead of us, giving them ample time to unload everything into the proper sectors before we reach the base." Clapping cupped hands to the outsides of his thighs, he performed a tidy about-face to address the movers, causing them to jump. "You men clear on your instructions? You all have your charts?"

The three day-laborers, each looking more dazed than the next, nodded and held up the diagrams. One of the men groaned and shifted from foot to foot. Another responded by sucking on his teeth. The tri-colored-arm man cursed under his breath in an unintelligible tongue.

"Good, then that does it. Time for the Drakes to shove off. Oorah!" the lieutenant cheered, the only person smiling other than Billy who let out an oorah of his own. A half-smile of self-satisfaction pulling at the corner of his mouth, the lieutenant gave his car keys a clamorous jangle. "Last call for the head!"

The movers plodded into the bungalow and grappled with the boxes in the living room, *accidentally* losing the diagrams.

Billy ran into the house, bumping into Pete again despite the wide-open space.

Pete's backpack slid off his shoulder and onto the grass as he kneaded his rammed arm.

My next invention's gonna be something that electrocutes him every time he does that.

The insistent kaah of the circling hawk pulled Pete's mind off creative modes of retaliation. Shielding his eyes from the unusually bright sun, he looked up to view the broad-winged bird that carried something dripping in its beak.

It's that bird again! And now it's hovering overhead like a vulture waiting for me to die or something. Jeez, I hate that bird ... Hey, that looks like the letter Mom tried to give me. I wonder if—

"You want this packed?" the man with the tri-color skin asked, holding up Pete's backpack.

"How many times have I told you not to leave your things lying around, Junior?"

"Sorry, sir." Pete tried to act nonchalant as he took the bag from the man. But he involuntarily shuddered at the up-close sight of the mover's piecemeal arm as the fellow slid his sleeve down over the shield-and-sword tattoo on his sallow forearm.

Once his backpack was firmly in his grasp, Pete willed his feet to move toward the car. He'd been dreading the long drive, especially the idea of being stuck in the back seat with his increasingly insufferable brother who had a penchant for putting Pete in headlocks, inserting spit-laden fingers in Pete's ears, and wiping off his own dirty hands on Pete's otherwise clean clothing.

Within minutes, all were buckled in and motoring toward the highway, the vehicle's trunk fastidiously pre-packed and gas tank filled.

"Damn bird's following us again," the lieutenant muttered, eying the hawk overhead through the windshield. "Probably looking for a handout. You boys didn't feed it, did you?"

"No way! I wouldn't get near that thing if you paid me!" Pete said.

Billy extracted the slingshot from his back pocket while feeling around the floor for something to use as ammunition. "Bet I can knock it out of the sky in one shot."

"You'll do no such thing, young man!" Cassie admonished. "Oh look, it has something in its beak."

"Trash, no doubt. Damn nuisance."

The hawk dropped Pete's waterlogged letter onto the windshield, changed course, and flapped away.

With the dexterity of a fly fisherman, the lieutenant worked the wipers until he was able to maneuver the dripping mass to the driver's side of the glass. He then rolled down the window, grabbed the letter, squeezed the water out of it, and flung the parchment onto the highway, all the while maintaining the speed limit.

Pete peered out the back window and watched as the family car pulled away from the soggy missive that looked like nothing more than a splat of oatmeal marked by a single tire track.

I sure would've liked to see what was in that letter.

He slumped in his seat and opened his backpack seeking solace. Therein, he espied a pad of half-used graph paper, a 0.9 mechanical pencil, a T-square, a portable cassette player with earphones, Fritos, chocolate covered raisins, and Butter Rum Lifesavers—all the things he deemed vital for surviving a road trip with his family sans homicide.

While Pete wrangled with a Lifesaver wrapper, a black widow crept out of his backpack and onto his arm.

"Aagh!" Pete screeched, leaning away from the spider, his arm frozen.

Billy tossed jellybeans at the arachnid. "Isn't that one of those poisonous spiders?"

"Black widows are venomous, not poisonous, Billy," the lieutenant corrected.

"Get it off me! Get it off me!"

"Don't act so dramatic, Junior. It's only a tiny bug. Just roll down your window and flick it off."

Pete furiously cranked down his window and, using his T-square, swatted the spider out onto the highway, manically rolling the window back up thereafter, lest the creature somehow return, seeking vengeance.

"I didn't know this region had black widows," Cassie remarked.

"It doesn't," the lieutenant said.

Pete zipped his backpack closed and crossed his arms. "Why does this stuff always happen to me?"

Billy picked a half-stepped-on jelly bean off the floor and popped it into his mouth. "It's like that weird witchy lady outside the store told you the day of the eclipse. She said the sun would go out and that it would be your fault."

"Now, Billy, you know better than to say such things," Cassie chided.

"It's true! You were there! She grabbed Pete's arm and looked him straight in the eye." Billy clamped a meaty hand around Pete's wrist and leaned in, dropping his voice to an overtly raspy whisper. "She said you're cursed to see things worse than your worst nightmares."

Pete's mouth went dry, and the bones in his wrist hurt from Billy's too-tight grip. "Cut it out! You don't know what you're talking about."

Billy let go and stuck his tongue out. "Do so know. I remember exactly what she said. 'P.J. will shatter the sun.' You better not do anything to the sun, Pete, or I swear I'll sock you. I hate winter!"

The lieutenant glanced at Pete in the rearview mirror and cleared his throat. "Junior, that woman was mentally deranged. There's no such thing as being cursed."

Pete surreptitiously rubbed his wrist then stowed his backpack under the backseat with a sullen shove.

Easy for you to say, you're not the one who's cursed!

CHAPTER THREE – THE DUBIOUS DINER

{Kapta Fui}

The car engine went silent, waking Pete just enough for him to worry about what he might face when he opened his eyes.

"Are we here?" he mumbled, trying to figure out when he dozed off.

His father turned his wrist over to consult his jumbo watch, the light glinting off the timepiece's glass face blasting Pete in the eye like a laser. "If by *here* you mean Uncle Dabney's famous Pigs in a Blanket Family Style Restaurant, yes. If you mean the new base, you're about ninety-three hours short."

"Yeah, dummy," Billy added, socking Pete's still-sore shoulder.

Yep, electrocution – definitely.

For the Drakes, the meal was business as usual. For the diner staff, it was a living nightmare.

The lieutenant insisted on switching tables more than once, complaining how smudged the tabletops were and griping about the condition of the booth upholstery. He demanded all of the hermetically sealed utensils be replaced with *clean* ones, and he sent back his wife's dessert order because it wasn't exactly the way *he* would've liked it.

Pete tuned out the commotion by his usual means, retreating into his head to design a *doodad*, the term he used to describe his favorite inventions—machines that involved complicated actions conducted by various mechanical parts all intended to perform a simple task. His original term for his proposed line of wunder-widgets was *doohickeys*, but he changed it to doo*dad*s, hoping his inventions would make his own *dad* proud. (The fact Billy made fun of the word *hickey* may have weighed into the decision as well.)

At six years of age, Pete had entered a science fair with The Scrammer, a contrivance he put together to scramble eggs at the flip of a switch. He'd meant the name to be The Scrambler, but couldn't fully enunciate the word, and his mother found his childlike pronunciation endearing, so the Scrammer moniker stuck. Employing a turntable, reflex hammer, flare, pie tin, and paint-can shaker, his creation was a cinch to win the fair's coveted Gold Volcano trophy along with a two-year subscription to *Safety First*—a moralistic science-themed comicbook series for kids.

His father had insisted on tying The Scrammer to the car's roof rack, disregarding Pete's and Cassie's pleas to stow it in the back of the station wagon.

The contraption made the trip intact. But in removing it from the car, the lieutenant was foiled by one of his own masterfully executed no-slip knots, and he inadvertently broke a large piece off the Scrammer.

Pete burst out weeping.

"Just tape it back on, Junior. You brought duct tape, didn't you?"

The little lad's tears flew in a semi-circle as he shook his head.

"For cryin' out loud, what sort of cockamamie builder doesn't carry duct tape with him?"

Tech lesson learned.

When showtime came, Pete's pride and joy was disqualified for failure to operate. No trophy for Team Drake.

Life lesson learned.

That was the last such competition the lieutenant allowed Pete to enter, for reasons the young inventor had yet to discover.

His current doodad was designed to make his existence as a teenage vassal substantially easier. He dubbed it the Auto-Scrub, a sort of do-it-yourself mechanized device for washing the exterior of an automobile—a lilliputian-sized automobile, mind you.

"P.J. … Pete … Peyton." Cassie lightly touched his arm.

"Aaagghhh!"

"Didn't mean to startle you, but we have to go. Your brother and dad are already out the door. You can resume your inventing when we get to the car."

Pete grabbed the shoulder strap of his backpack and grudgingly scooted out of the booth, convinced the family would never make it through the remainder of the trip without some sort of catastrophic blow-up or calamity. Taking halting steps, he moved toward the door, fiddling with the contents of his backpack, his mother prodding him forward.

"Wazzak!" cried a bubbly teenage girl sporting vintage sunglasses and a swinging ponytail, jumping to the side to avoid a head-on collision with Pete as they passed each other in the doorway.

"Oh, sorry," Pete said, toying with the stuck zipper on his backpack as his feet continued in the general direction of the car where Billy sat leaning on the horn.

"Just some barmpot I almost knocked into," the girl commented, seemingly to no one. "No worries, no one suspects anything. These clueless Q-zers won't know what hit 'em, or should I say *who* hit 'em."

Pete stopped short, his mouth agape.

"What's wrong, P.J.? Another spider?"

"No, were you listening to that girl?" he whispered, hunching to be less visible, his eyes darting in search of whomever the girl was talking to.

"What girl?" Cassie nudged Pete out to the parking lot. "Walk and talk at the same time, P.J. And if you're referring to the young lady at the entrance, the answer is no. I was not eavesdropping on her conversation. And you shouldn't have been either!"

"I didn't mean to, but that's not the point. She sounded like she was plotting something—"

Another blare of the car horn forced Pete to shelve his conspiracy theories.

"On the double!" the lieutenant called, standing beside the open car door and giving a few quick taps to his watch buttons. "You've put us six minutes behind schedule, Junior."

"Sorry, sir," Pete called back, jogging as he prepared to picture both his father and brother in circus clown regalia crammed into a VW Bug with dozens of their clown-car crewmates. But for once, picturing his father looking absurd had lost its appeal.

After returning to his designated seat, Pete stowed his backpack out of his brother's reach, then buckled his seatbelt with one hand while holding his shoulder with the other hand in case of another punch from Billy—a wise move as it turned out.

Less than five minutes into the next leg of their trip, Pete reached the point he could take his brother's juvenility and his father's sermonizing no longer.

His cassette player and earphones did little to mute the lieutenant's droning litany of upcoming entries on the travel timetable, and every time Pete tried to make a design notation on his notepad, he found himself transcribing his father's words. The lieutenant had just gotten to the part where at 0800 hours they would check out of their motel room and go to the on-site coffee shop for eggs, bacon, and two slices of toast, when the car hopped and veered sharply.

"Careful, Peter," Cassie cautioned.

"That wasn't me. It was the road!" The lieutenant pulled over to the shoulder to turn on the radio as cars zigzagged precariously toward them.

"But Dad, you're gonna make us later," Billy remarked from his half of the backseat where he'd already amassed a small mountain of debris and refuse.

"Not now, Billy!" his father snapped, spinning the radio knob in search of a voice. "Why can't I get a damn signal? We're not that far from the city … Ah, yahtzee!"

> **"… still searching for an explanation. Experts are stymied as to the cause of this unusual phenomenon, but they assure the public there is no reason to panic. You can all go about your day as normal …"**

"Good enough for me." The lieutenant put the car back in gear and pulled into traffic as if nothing unnatural or disturbing had happened.

Pete stared out the back window in the direction of the diner and the dubious girl he encountered there, convinced something was amiss and she was part of it.

"Eight minutes behind schedule," his father complained, swerving as he tried to program his mega watch while steering.

Cassie turned around to face her sons with a reassuring smile. "See, boys, there's nothing to worry about."

Pete's view out the back window suggested otherwise. All at once, storm clouds converged over the area, swirling menacingly and pummeling the car with hail. A fissure split the highway open, unzipping the asphalt behind them.

The hawk from home followed, its wings battered by the hail, the mangled parchment letter in its beak. The sky fractured into bolts of raw electricity as the heavens slammed together in a world-rending cymbal crash that vibrated through the station wagon's chassis and sent the hawk into a tailspin. Then the rain started in earnest.

Pete's eyes widened. *But where's the hawk?*

CHAPTER FOUR – A CUSTODIAN'S WORK IS NEVER DONE

{Kapta Ud}

Pete's eyeballs burned and itched. He'd hardly slept throughout the journey, having forced himself to stay awake and alert to signs of aberrant activity. To his relief, nothing out of the ordinary had occurred since the diner episode and convulsive storm. The remainder of the drive was uneventful, and for better or worse, the ominous hawk was nowhere in sight.

The new town's monotonous streets appeared idyllically conventional—the perfect match for Pete's milquetoast public persona. Maybe his mother was right. Maybe this latest move would present a grand adventure. In his book, that would amount to unlimited time alone to create spectacular inventions in a household free of turmoil or strife.

"Oh look, P.J., the city swimming pool," Cassie chirped, pointing down the street. "Perhaps you can take lessons."

The very mention of swimming caused Pete's throat to constrict, not in a nervous sort of way—more in an I-can't-breathe-because-I'm-drowning sort of way.

His experiences with water that could not be controlled by a faucet had been uniformly disastrous. From being pantsed at the pool, to belly-flopping in front of cheerleader Stacey Larkspur, to ear infections, to his inability to master any stroke beyond the dog paddle, one thing was clear—Pete would never swim for Olympic gold.

His general lack of athletic prowess failed to give him pause. He had no interest in sports, and by all accounts, the feeling was mutual.

Maybe if I pretend I wanna join some club or start a paper route or something, Mom will forget about swimming.

A siren and flashing lights pursued the car. Pete instinctively held his backpack over his head for protection.

"What now?" the lieutenant groused, pulling over to let an ambulance pass.

The emergency vehicle came to an abrupt stop in front of the pool—siren off, lights still flashing. A pair of paramedics burst out of the back doors, snapping open a gurney before charging through the gates where a crowd wearing bathing suits hovered over a motionless body.

No more swimming. Case closed!

Aside from the aquatic crisis, the paramedic interlude proved beneficial to Pete. Ever since his mother's last birthday, he'd unsuccessfully endeavored to fabricate a pop-up bed tray as a gift for her. Observing the functionality of the medical gurney, Pete's mind clicked onto the streamlined design solution that had eluded him for months.

At least one good thing came out of this road trip.

The lieutenant clenched both his jaw and the steering wheel as the family drove up to their empty new home ahead of schedule. "Where are they? They should have been finished unloading by now."

With maternal diplomacy, Cassie suggested the family head to the cafeteria to grab something to eat while waiting for the wayward movers. The lieutenant initially balked at the idea of dining during the time scheduled for unpacking, then he admitted he was hungry and that Cassie's plan was an efficient use of time.

The moment the lieutenant's hot entrée arrived, so did the moving truck.

Two of the movers schlepped into the dining hall, taking their time as though they hadn't a care in the world. The man with the tri-colored arm was not with them. "We saw your note on your front door saying you'd be here," the head mover drawled, note in hand.

"Is the other man unloading?"

"Other man's gone."

"Gone! I hired three of you. Where did he go?"

"Couldn't tell ya. Got attacked at a rest stop by a ferocious bird. Ran off and never came back."

Pete nearly choked on his dill pickle spear. *Ferocious bird?*

"Damn!" Lt. Drake threw his napkin down like a gauntlet with a mumbled vow to vent his hunger and vexation on the labor force. After pressing a noisy series of watch buttons, he goose-stepped toward the exit and out of sight.

The two men followed, albeit at a much more leisurely pace.

"Could we please get that to go?" Cassie asked a busboy, pointing at the lieutenant's congealing entrée.

While Billy constructed a moat out of his mashed potatoes, Cassie swallowed the last bite of her French dip sandwich along with a trio of pills. Pete's eyes boggled—one pill was business as usual; three was an alarm bell. Getting up from the table, she wrung her hands as she informed the boys she would be heading to the bungalow. They were to stay out of the line of fire. She'd fetch them when the coast was clear.

Billy, a bloodhound when it came to sniffing out trouble and troublemakers, rounded up some kids in the dining hall and recommended they throw rocks at glass bottles. His new compatriots considered the plan inspired.

Pete left them to their hooliganism and ventured into an open adjoining lounge. There he found a large unoccupied armchair and settled in for some serious gadget brainstorming. As he'd come to expect, the space was similar to the rec room at the last base and the one before it.

The people looked the same. The furnishings looked the same. The place even smelled the same. Everything was the same, except everything was new—that is, new to him. All too soon he'd be forced to brave a new school, new teachers, and most egregious of all, new kids.

He disliked change as a rule and disliked conflict even more. Change brought the potential for conflict. With new people, that potentiality turned to probability.

Thankfully, he wouldn't have to put up with any such socializing twaddle this time around. He'd already made up his mind to avoid all fraternizing at the impending school, viewing his new-kid-in-town status as a fresh opportunity to pump up his powers of social invisibility and dodge bullies. Not only would his deliberate lack of friends appease his overprotective father, it would afford more time for inventing and tinkering. Yes, something good could come out of this move yet.

By bedtime, the Drakes had unpacked and put away their essentials per the lieutenant's detailed instructions. Pete needed no direction to be in compliance with his father's organizational regulations. Each of the six housing units Pete remembered inhabiting was laid out the exact same way. With eyes closed, he could easily locate his toothbrush or find the refrigerator to sneak a forbidden midnight snack. That night, he couldn't wait to close his eyes—simply to catch up on sleep.

* * *

Pete's wake-up alarm went off the first morning in the new house just as it always did, and he started the day just as he always did—he put on his slippers, slid into his robe, and traipsed out to the breakfast bar. During his trek, he questioned the relevance of the robe. Weren't pajamas sufficient apparel for breakfast at home with the family? And what about slippers? Were they really necessary given he wore socks to bed? These were the questions with which he greeted each day—questions he kept to himself so as not to have to endure his father's homiletic answers.

As usual, his parents were already seated, or rather, his father was seated reading the newspaper and nursing a mug of black coffee. His mother was standing in the kitchen, humming as she prepared the meal outlined on the monthly menu posted on the refrigerator door. Mom's famous orange-vanilla French toast made the morning list, garnished with a powdered sugar snowflake and served with blackberry syrup, a sausage patty, and orange sections.

"Billyyyy," the lieutenant called in the direction of the boys' rooms.

As the walls shook with the thunder of a runaway bison charging through the hallway, Pete took the precaution of shielding his plate with one arm and scooting his chair away from Billy's. Billy had a way with food—a way that resulted in more of it ending up on and around him than in him. Before the Tasmanian devil had taken his first bite, Cassie was at the broom closet, selecting a hand-held whisker and dustpan as her weapons in the battle of the Billy.

Pete kept his eyes on his plate, attempting to disregard the fact his father had been peering at him over the top of a newspaper for several discomfiting seconds.

"You all done with breakfast?" the lieutenant asked.

Pete nodded, chewing the last of his sausage patty quickly to get back to his room and work on the pop-up bed tray idea for his mother.

"Good! Then wash your breakfast things and put them in the drying rack. And don't forget the pots and pans. Lord knows your mother does enough cleaning up after you two."

Says the man who's never cleaned a dish in his life.

"When you're through, I want you to do some recon and get the lay of the land. School starts in just three days, and I expect you sharp and ready come Tuesday, Junior. Last thing we need is a repeat of the last town's first day at school. Take Billy and scout out the new school ... That's an order."

"Yes, sir," the siblings said in unison, each with differing levels of enthusiasm.

Pete collected dirty dishes and utensils while the kitchen sink filled with soapy water. He was just lowering the stack of dishes into the sink when Billy bumped him out of the way and turned the tap on full blast. Billy waved his plate under the torrent, splashing Pete before leaving his still-dirty and now dripping dishware on the kitchen counter.

Pete took a zen breath, dunked a sponge in the sudsy water, and scrubbed.

He was painfully aware that the compulsory recon mission would put the kibosh on his plans for a morning design session. Add to that, he was stuck on KP duty and was about to be saddled with Billy. To assuage his frustration, he pictured his father reading the paper wearing nothing but skivvies. The mental picture gave Pete the willies and made him feel worse.

I need a new survival technique.

Pete slung his tan canvas backpack over one shoulder and exited the bungalow's front door, dressed in his usual tan corduroy jeans, tan suede Wallabees shoes, and a plain tan tee—a shirt without a logo or design so as not to draw attention. This was his signature ensemble, one he'd crafted to help him go unnoticed. Even his hair color matched.

He shambled to the end of the walkway, pausing to look for a directional signpost that would point them toward the school. As expected, there was one on each corner of the lane—just as there had been at all the bases they'd lived on. Billy paid no heed to his big brother or the signs and ran pell-mell down the road, presumably to find or cause mischief.

Pete watched in satisfaction as Billy rounded a corner and disappeared, leaving Pete by himself.

This morning's looking up already.

Ambling toward the small community's sixth- through twelfth-grade school, Pete was struck by the intense colors of the scenery. The blue of the sky, the white of the clouds, the green of the trees, and the lush hues of the flowers had never looked so vibrant. Had the natural world always been so colorful, or was he experiencing something extraordinary? He concluded it was the former and vowed to be more appreciative of nature going forward.

When he arrived at the campus, he found it blessedly deserted. The buildings were nondescript and the grounds bereft of foliage—a stark contrast to the splendor of the neighboring area's vivid palette. A pair of side doors labeled Administration Office stood open, revealing nothing but a hallway even drabber than the building's exterior.

Pete ventured inside, planning to stay just long enough to get a basic idea of the school's layout before zipping home to enjoy his last homework-free weekend at the drafting table.

"Hello … Hello," he called, hoping no one would reply.

Please let there be no people. Please let there be no people.

One of the entry doors banged closed, causing him nearly to swallow his tongue. Continuing down the main corridor, he perused the myriad hand-painted banners announcing this, requesting that.

So many smiling faces I hope never to meet.

Lost in contemplation of display cases crowded with school trophies and memorabilia, he rounded a corner and walked right into the backside of a woman bending over a mop bucket.

The chubby worker's bum let out a toot, and she straightened up like a spring. "Hoh!"

Pete's face twisted in mortification as he struggled to find words to offer in apology. "Are you … okay?" was all he managed.

"Right as rain," she said, facing him and flashing a cheerful smile accented by cherubic dimples. "And all the better for seeing you."

"Me?"

Still smiling, she rolled up the sleeves of her khaki work shirt, then pulled hard on a lever extending from the bucket to squeeze the water from her mop. Working vigorously, she swabbed her way toward him. "Couldn't wait for school to start, eh?"

He backed up to evade the mop's advances, unsure how to respond. "Oh, well, I don't know yet. I just—"

"That was a joke, Peyton. What teenage boy wants to start school any earlier than he has to?"

"Oh, heh heh. Yeah, I've never much looked forward to the first day of school." After backing into a glass case, he turned around to walk beside the chipper janitor as she mopped in the direction of the entrance. The sunlight that filled the single open door served as a beacon of hope, offering the promise of escape back to the house.

"No one ever looks forward to summer ending … except for high school girls eager to show off their new wardrobes, of course."

"I wouldn't know. I've never been a high school student … or a girl."

"True," she said with a flourish of her mop. "Besides, your school has a uniform dress code. A rather stylish one, if you ask me."

Pete froze. "My dad didn't tell me anything about this school having uniforms. I don't have one. He's gonna kill me!" He tore into his thumbnail cuticles, his throat contracting as he spoke. "Somehow he'll find a way to make it like it's all my fault."

"Calm yourself, Peyton. Who said anything about *this* school?"

"Well … I mean …"

"I'm here with him now, syr."

Pete looked around in search of whomever she was addressing, but saw no one.

"I will, syr, the moment we're done. I understand." The woman placed her mop in the bucket and turned to face Pete squarely. "I think you better take a seat, Peyton. Life as you know it is about to turn upside down."

CHAPTER FIVE – THE OCADEMY

{Kapta Jai}

Unclear as to what was going on, but feeling surprisingly comfortable in the presence of a woman who talked to her mop, Pete followed her to the end of the hall. Dimples fully engaged, the janitorial worker gestured toward a row of terra-cotta-colored metal chairs lined against a bone-colored wall. Pete's knees bent automatically, obliging him to sit.

"How did you know my name was Peyton?" he asked, his heart rate and curiosity building.

"Oh, I'm sorry. Do you prefer Pete? Or perhaps P.J., as your mother calls you? I'm guessing you don't much care for being called Junior. Makes no sense, your father calling you Junior when his name's Peter and yours is Peyton."

"Mix-up on my birth certificate," he recited by rote, searching her face for a hint as to who she was and how she knew so much about him.

She chortled. "I'd call that more than just a mix-up. More of a clusterfail, if you ask me. But you're here now. That's what matters. Deora knows how long we've waited for you."

"Who are you?" he whispered.

She extended her hand in introduction. "I'm Etta."

He seesawed her pillowy fingers, regarding her in confounded silence as he waited for further explanation.

Pulling her hand back, she fanned herself. "Whewf, warm in here. Always is during the dog days." Bowing her head, she removed her turban-tied bandana, igniting an explosion of orange curls that sprang out in all directions. Using the bandana, she blotted the perspiration from her face as she spoke. "Sweaty business, being a Custodian."

"You're like no custodian *I've* ever met before."

"Why, thank you! I take that as a compliment. But you see, I'm not a Custodian for *this* school."

"Oh? Is there another one in town?"

She let out a long hearty laugh before answering. "Noooo. I'm from Omni."

He stared at her blankly.

"As in the Academy of Omniosophical Arts and Sciences."

His eyes glazed over.

"Don't tell me your parents never mentioned the Ocademy to you."

"My parents?"

"You *are* aware you have parents, yes?"

He nodded, the conversation getting away from him.

"I can understand why your father wouldn't talk about the Ocademy. Still sticks in his craw, I imagine, his application being denied. But surely Cassiopeia has told you stories."

"Who?"

"Your mother, silly mongoose."

"My mom's name is Cassie, not—"

"Short for Cassiopeia."

Pete gazed at her in frozen stupefaction.

Her smile faded. "Were you not put to bed at night hearing tales of the heroic Cassiopeia?"

Pete shook his head. "My parents used to read to me about the Three Little Pigs and Goldilocks and stuff, but nobody named Cassi-however-you-say it."

Etta slapped her thighs and stood, her angelic face having morphed into the sourmug of a bulldog. "Young man, I don't find your joking behavior at all amusing."

"Joking? I'm not joking – about anything. I swear, Miss, umm, Etta, I have no idea what you're talking about. As for joking, I'm not all that good at telling jokes."

She cocked her head and looked at him hard. "You're telling the truth."

"I know I am!"

"You'd make a lousy stand-up comic."

"Hey!"

"But this still doesn't explain how you know nothing about your legendary mother – how she came to the aid of that ravaged village."

"Legendary? Ma'am, I love my mom – a lot – but I think you got the wrong grownup. My mom is … well … she's just a mom. And she's a great mom – the best mom a kid could ask for. She makes all of my meals and washes my clothes—"

"Hmpph, you make her sound like a housemaid!" Etta jerked her chin and crossed her arms, jutting one leg out to the side for added indignation.

"She also makes really good milkshakes," Pete offered feebly.

Etta put her hands on her hips, pacing and grumbling.

This is why I dread meeting new people!

"I'm really sorry, ma'am. I didn't mean to upset you. I just think you've got my mom confused with someone else."

"Ha! I'd be more likely to confuse my own mother than to confuse yours. Every girl at the Ocademy wished they were her—every boy too, for that matter. We all idolized her."

Pete shrugged, at a loss for how to reply.

Etta dabbed her neck with the kerchief then wrapped her rebellious hair inside it once more. Her eyes darted in thought. "This is your father's doing. How did I not see it before? Of course he wouldn't want you to know. If he couldn't attend the Ocademy, why should you get to? That good-for-nothin' snake in the grass."

"That's how my dad treats me."

"Your own father treats you like a snake in the grass? How dare—"

"No, like a good-for-nothing. It's obvious he thinks *nothing* is all I'm good for."

The mercurial little woman sat next to him again, taking his hands in hers. "Peyton Drake, you are *not* good for nothing. You hear me? Why, you're good for – well – for everything! It's time we got you out of this place – before you're too far gone."

"What? Leave? I can't leave. We just got into town. And I start school here in three days."

"You start school in *two* days and certainly not here! Now then, Leon and I will meet you at the portal at six a.m. the day after tomorrow."

"Portal. Wait, what?"

"Yes, at six a.m. day after next."

"But I can't—"

"You *can* as long as you have authorization from a parent. Here's a copy of your induction letter." She raised one hip to retrieve a flattened wax-sealed scroll from her back pocket. "I'm sure Cassiopeia will be thrilled to inscribe it."

Hey, that looks like the seal on the letter Dad threw away!

His hand hesitating at first, Pete took the parchment and carefully dislodged the seal. His pancreas throbbed as he scanned the text. Words tumbled out of his mouth without his permission. "What is all this? Are *you* the one trying to pull some sort of weird joke on *me*?"

"Certainly not! And if you'll settle down, I can explain it all."

Pete remained in his seat while his eyes searched for the nearest exit sign. Clearly, the lady was bonkers.

"You see, well, first off, Omni, since you don't know, is the only interdimensional school in the Omniverse at this time. It was founded —" She gasped, her face stretching in worry, her voice dropping to a hush. "Good Gobfinkle, they're looking for you."

"Who? ... That girl from the diner yesterday? I knew there was something fishy about her! I tried to tell—"

"No, your parents, or rather your father." Etta looked frenetically in every direction then grabbed Pete's shoulders and lifted him onto his feet as effortlessly as if he were a package of marshmallows.

"Where is he? How do you know?" Pete asked in a frantic yodel.

"Because I know! Now take this." She folded the academy letter and stuffed it in Pete's shirt pocket, glancing right and left down the hallways like a spectator at a tennis match. "Remember, you need to discuss this with your parents – correction, your *mother*, since you need parental approval. But for Deora's sake do *not* tell your brother – or anyone else for that matter! Now go, before your father comes here searching for you."

Pete nodded and raced out the door. When he got to the street, he looked back over his shoulder. The school doors were shut tight, the glass dark and dead as if no one had stepped inside all summer. He kept running, his pace marking time with the bewildering thoughts that bounced through his mind. His skin tightened with the encroaching certainty that his days of anonymity were over.

CHAPTER SIX – FISHING

{Kapta Etts}

Pete burst full speed through the new bungalow's front door, stopping just shy of smashing into the living room's back wall.

The lieutenant sat in his favorite armchair, smiling nonchalantly.

Something's wrong with this picture. Why is Dad smiling? Does he know about Etta?

"Junior, good. You're here. No irksome fowls or damn messengers with mis-addressed missives at this new base, I'm happy to report."

Huh?

"You bring your brother with you?"

Pete shook his head, standing bent over with his hands on his knees, too winded to speak.

"For cryin' out loud, do I have to do everything around here myself?" His father marched out the front door in search of Billy, scowling, muttering, and savagely pressing buttons on his watch.

That's more like it.

Cassie entered, yawning. "You feeling all right, P.J.?" she asked, putting a comforting hand on his back.

He peered up into her smiling face, studying it for signs of the heroine Etta described; but for all his mental straining, he still saw only Mom. Boldly, he decided to test the waters.

"Hey, Mom … I'm really looking forward to attending the academy. Did you enjoy it when you were there?"

Her eyes shimmered, and for a moment Pete thought he saw a spark flicker behind her pupils.

"Oh yes, I always loved school – the mesmerizing teachers and fascinating classes, the pageantry of the big game and galas, all the friends I knew so well back then …" She paused, putting one hand over heart, the other to her lips, then walked into the kitchen. "What say I bake some cookies?"

Pete scratched at his thumbnails.

This isn't working.

He and his mother had an unflappable rapport, and he'd always been able to talk to her about anything. Even so, he saw the road to answers crumbling before him like the highway behind them at the diner.

Before launching in again, he looked out the front window to confirm the lieutenant was nowhere in sight. "Yeah, meeting people from other dimensions must've been pretty crazy."

He held his breath, prickling in anticipation.

"Come again, sweetheart?" she called.

Drat!

He went into the kitchen and opened his mouth to repeat the question, but instead, fearing interruption by his father or Billy, he went straight for the jugular.

"So, Mom, what can you tell me about Omni?"

She wheeled around and locked eyes with him, massaging the base of her skull.

His hands went into cuticle-attack mode, and had she not replied a second later, his thumbs might have been picked to the bone.

"Peanut butter chocolate chip."

"What's that?" Pete whispered, suspecting she was speaking in some sort of academy code.

"That's the flavor I think I should bake – peanut butter chocolate chip. Whaddaya say?" She turned and waltzed over to the broom closet to take a clean, well-worn apron off a hook, humming as she tied the pinafore around her slim waist.

Pete leaned back flat against the refrigerator, powerless to do anything but observe dumbly as his mother deftly pulled ingredients from the pantry shelves.

I surrender.

"Anyone seen that boy?!" the lieutenant roared, back from his fruitless Billy hunt.

"'Fraid not, hon."

Pete shook his head, his mind grasping for a way to regroup after striking out with his mother.

Maybe if I could get her off her medication, she'd remember ...

"I tell you, those sons of yours will be the end of me." The lieutenant roughly removed his boots then placed them punctiliously by the door. "I'm going to wash up."

Alone again with his mother, Pete tried another ploy. "So ... Cassiopeia ..."

"Yes, P.J.?" she replied with typical affability.

Pete gasped, uncertain as to what to say next.

The front door flew open, and Billy tore in.

Pete jumped in startlement, smacking the back of his head on the edge of the kitchen cupboard.

Billy leaned against the door as he locked it and slammed the deadbolt into place, then dropped to the floor to spy out the front window from behind the bottom edge of a curtain.

The lieutenant returned to the room to find his vile offspring back in the nest. "There's my little Marine!"

"Not so little anymore," Cassie noted as Billy put his thick hands on his bulbous knees to stand.

Billy smirked and falumped onto the sofa, grabbing a handful of chocolates from the crystal *guest bowl* on the coffee table. Putting his feet up on the table, he knocked his brick-like shoe against the delicate bowl, causing it to ring as he carelessly littered the couch with candy wrappers.

Dad would throttle me if I put my feet up like that and ate the guest treats.

"Look at the size of those feet. You're gonna make a fine defensive tackle one of these days, son," the lieutenant said, nearly salivating with pride. "Isn't that right, cupcake?"

"It certainly is," Cassie called from the kitchen. "I have no doubt both of the boys have bright athletic futures ahead of them. You know, P.J.'s swimming has been coming along, slow but steady – and no more holding his nose!"

Pete made a peculiar noise that sounded like he swallowed backwards. *I sure hope the academy can get me out of swimming.*

The lieutenant indulged a contemptuous chuckle. "Swimming?! Well that's not exactly football, now is it, Cassie?"

She replied in a pleasant, yet factual tone. "No, it's not, Peter. It's swimming."

It was Pete who chuckled this time, then coughed to disguise the fact as he exchanged a faint smile with his mother. She was all right by him, and he couldn't wait to learn more about the mysterious *Cassiopeia* and her days at the academy.

Once the cookies came out of the oven, it was time to prepare the evening meal. Per usual, the lieutenant and Billy retreated to the carport to play ping-pong, thereby dodging any duties associated with domesticity.

Pete took a seat at the breakfast bar, keen to extract more information from his mother. "I met a really nice custodian today …"

"That's good to hear. The people who maintain public buildings get so little acknowledgment. Think of all the effort they put into making things nice for the rest of us."

"Well, she wasn't exactly *that* kind of custodian." He leaned forward to analyze her expression for clues, nearly falling off his barstool.

"No? What other kind is there?"

"You know … the *dimensional* kind," he said quietly, then held his breath in preparation of the big moment.

"Now, P.J. if you're going to help, how about you actually *do* something," she returned, moving the discussion down a new and decidedly more mundane track.

He flopped his chest onto the counter, expelling his breath like a tire going flat.

How did she do that? She totally changed the subject!

He needed to find a way to keep the conversation going and get back to academy topics, even if it meant culinary servitude. "Okay. Like what?"

"Pardon?"

"You said you wanted me to do something in the kitchen?"

"Did I?" She closed her eyes and pinched the bridge of her nose, mumbling inaudibly. She then removed the pillbox from her pocket and opened it, only to stare at it for a long moment before clapping it closed without having ingested a tablet.

Pete scrunched his toes in his shoes to help fight the urge to gasp. He'd never seen her forego her medication, but this was not the time to bring it up, exciting as it was.

Cassie pressed her palms against the sides of her head for several seconds, then dropped her hands and turned to face Pete with a breezy smile, her eyes brighter than usual. "How about you help with the salad."

He viewed her intently, doing his best to play it cool. "Okay … how?"

"Start by going to the fridge and taking out all the fixings you like."

"Sounds easy enough."

He opened the refrigerator and combed its contents for things that looked salady. After inspecting the vegetable drawer, he pulled out two kinds of lettuce, carrots, kale, celery, cucumber, sprouts, avocado, and a red onion—then put the kale back.

With one arm loaded up to his chin with produce, he used his free hand to grab a chunk of cheese to add to the pile, plus a bottle of salad dressing, and finally a large jar of artichoke hearts, using his foot to close the refrigerator door. As he turned to place the groceries on the counter, the artichoke jar slipped from his grasp and plunged toward the floor.

Cassie casually stuck out her hand and caught the heavy jar midair.

She and Pete stared at each other, both momentarily dumbstruck.

Pete bent over the counter and let the cradled items roll out onto the tiled surface. Cassie placed the glass container on the counter, tucked her hair behind her ear, and returned to her dinner preparations, mumbling to herself again.

Pete's pulse galloped. "You okay, Mom?"

"Yes, thanks. I'm fine. I'll be fine. Just a little rattled is all. You know, settling into a new place …"

Pete's mouth twisted.

I'm not buying it. Mom's settled into plenty of new *places without ever being* rattled.

She ripped pieces of lettuce, avoiding eye contact. "Why don't you go tinker a little, P.J. I can take it from here."

"You sure, Mom?"

"Yes. I could use some time to myself anyway … to get used to this new kitchen."

"Okay, Mom. Whatever you say." He stared at her more closely, sensing she was on the verge of revealing something.

"P.J.?"

This is it!

He held onto the edge of the counter for support and relaxed his knees to keep them from locking. "Yeah, Mom?"

"If you could set the dinner table, that would be a big help."

His whole body wilting in defeat, he slogged to the sideboard to gather the napkins and cutlery. When he reached over the breakfast bar to grab the salt and pepper shakers on the countertop, he noticed his mother was chopping the vegetables with forced, haphazard strokes—not the norm for Cassie Drake who possessed knife-wielding skills that would put a teppanyaki chef to shame. Pete worried her erraticism was his fault—that he'd distressed her in some way.

Silently, he put the dinnerware on the table, then headed to his room to give his mother some breathing space—for the time being. An hour later, Cassie called the troops to dinner. Pete emerged from his room with a first draft drawing of a pop-up bed tray in the hope of making her smile.

"This is exactly what I need!" Cassie gushed, kissing Pete on the cheek. "P.J., you're my hero."

The lieutenant snorted. "Junior a hero? Not likely, cupcake – not as long as he's living under this roof."

The comment had little effect on Pete. He was used to his father's derision—especially when it came to Pete's inventions.

Cassie carefully folded the paper and slid it into her apron pocket. "Well I love it."

As the Drake men took their seats, she placed the salad bowl and a basket of rolls on the table, apparently no longer *rattled.* Cassie made another trip to the kitchen and returned carrying a casserole straight from the oven. "Who's hungry?" she asked, smiling, one of her eyes twitching.

The lieutenant tucked a corner of his dinner napkin into the open neck of his shirt while Billy banged his utensils on the table as he always did until served.

Cassie set the casserole down on a trivet, then plunged a large serving spoon into the dish's center and scooped a hefty portion onto a plate. "That's odd," she said, eying the gelatinous mass. "It should be bubbling hot." Removing one of the oven mitts, she lowered her bare hand to touch the casserole.

"Careful, Mom!" Pete warned. "You'll burn yourself."

"Your mother knows what she's doing, Junior."

Cassie poked a finger deep into the mixture. "Good Gobfinkle, it's cold as an Aurelean moon!"

Pete wheezed at hearing the words *Good Gobfinkle*—the same phrase Etta had uttered.

The lieutenant bolted upright, banging his knees on the underside of the table. "What did you say?!" With white-knuckled fingers, he clutched the tabletop's edge, his hands shaking so fiercely the utensils and glasses on the table clattered.

A chill shot up Pete's spine as Etta's words streaked through his mind. This was it. This was the moment *his life turned upside down.*

CHAPTER SEVEN – CRISIS AVERTED

{Kapta Rreh}

Pete's eyes felt like leaden pinballs as they darted back and forth between his parents, searching their faces for some sort of explanation.

Billy followed his mother's lead and poked the cold noodle mélange with his fingers. He then ate it with his fingers.

The spoon in Cassie's hand toppled to the floor. She sank into her chair, shivering. Casting an imploring look at her husband, she hugged herself and rocked. "What's happening to me, Peter?"

Lt. Drake rushed to her side and kissed her cheek tenderly. "Nothing. Not one darn thing, cupcake. You'll be fine. You just need more medication. Don't you worry. I'll take care of everything. Why don't we get you to bed." He helped her to her feet then calmly turned to Pete. "Junior, call for pizza."

"Pizza!" Billy cheered, oblivious to the tension in the room.

The lieutenant put an arm around Cassie to escort her to their bedroom. "*Now*, Junior!"

The picture of his mother collapsing into her chair, so visibly distraught, got Pete right in the gut—a spot adjacent to his pancreas. He careened his way to the refrigerator, his sense of equilibrium gone. His eyes refused to focus, and he found it impossible to read the list of approved vendors posted on the appliance door.

He misdialed the telephone more than once, waking a family's baby and calling a non-English-speaking dry cleaner before connecting with the pizzeria. Under different circumstances, the unexpected luxury of ordering pizza would have been the highlight of his day, but it held little interest for him at the moment.

"Hi, my dad wants me to order a pizza … Yes, I can hold."

As he listened to a repeating selection of catchy jingles and promotional offers, one thought ran over and over in his mind. *She said, "Good Gobfinkle," same as Etta.*

After placing the order—a basic pepperoni and mushroom combination per the lieutenant's standing mandate—Pete headed down the hall to look in on his mother. Still wobbly, he held his arms out to the side to keep from bumping into the walls.

The atmosphere in the tidy room was calm as Cassie lay on the pristinely made bed, still wearing her apron.

Pete crept up to her side and knelt, examining her face. Though she was paler than normal, to him she'd never looked more beautiful.

I wonder what she's thinking.

His father ambled in from the master bathroom holding a glass of water and a large bottle of pills. Upon catching sight of Pete, he glowered. "What are you doing here, Junior?!"

Good question.

"Uh, I just wanted to tell you I ordered the pizza and it will be here in about forty-five minutes."

"Oh, all right. Good work. Now run along and wait on the porch for the deliveryman … and take Billy with you."

"Yes, sir." Pete exited the room, his wooziness subsiding as he worked his brain to come up with an excuse to speak to his mother privately again later. The rest of the house was silent—never a good sign when Billy was left alone. Pete's first instinct was to check the stovetop's gas burners to see if Billy had turned them on for sport. To his relief, Billy was in the dining room, his face buried in the cold casserole dish. "Dad says to wait outside for the pizza guy."

"Pizza!" Billy cheered, dropping the glass dish onto the table with a thud before lumbering out the front door.

Pete followed Billy outside and plopped onto the porch swing, his mind still reeling.

As was the Drake tradition, a bench swing sat on the front porch of the home. It was a sacred place to Pete as it was the one spot where his parents seemed truly relaxed—a spot where they connected without an undercurrent of anxiety. When swinging, they would hold hands, rub noses, coo and cuddle. It was the only setting where the lieutenant would let his guard down and laugh.

Pete pulled a peeling chip of paint off the bench, then tried to stick it back on.

I wish they'd swing more often.

Growing tired of watching Billy smash nocturnal insects, Pete sidled down the long porch to peek through his parents' bedroom window. There wasn't much to see. His mother was sitting up and looking at her folded hands. His father sat on the edge of the bed next to her, speaking just low enough to prevent Pete from making out what he was saying. When the lieutenant stood, Pete scurried back to the bench, swinging as if he'd been there for ages.

A moment later, the screen door creaked, just like all their previous homes' screen doors creaked.

Two exaggerated boot stomps indicated his father stopped in the doorway.

"Is Mom okay?" Pete asked.

The lieutenant assumed a parade rest stance. "Of course she is. Moving can be very stressful is all."

You're tellin' me!

"What were those things she was saying … sir?" Pete gripped the arm of the wooden bench, steadying himself against his own audacity.

"Nothing … gibberish … She was just dehydrated … Makes you hallucinate and say all sorts of senseless things."

Whatever was going on with his mother, it was obvious to Pete his father was in on it—and Pete was determined to get to the bottom of it.

A tiny blue car topped by a large lighted sign in the shape of a pizza slice whizzed around the corner and skidded to a stop in front of the house.

"He's too early. Get inside, Junior!" The lieutenant pulled Pete off the bench and tossed him through the door. Standing guard in front of it, he shouted to the driver. "You'll never take my son. Ya hear me?!"

I think Dad's losing his mind.

A toothy delivery boy wearing an All-Star Pizzeria cap skipped up the walkway. "Pizza order for Drake?"

"That can't be ours. It's much too soon." The lieutenant widened his stance, his face locked in a distrustful scowl. "Who are you? A messenger?"

The boy took all four front steps in a single stride and held the box out for the lieutenant's acceptance. "You're in luck, mister. Someone ordered this then changed their mind after it was in the oven. It just came out, and it's still hot."

"Used pizza?!" The veins in the lieutenant's neck surfaced and changed color as he fumed. "You expect us to eat someone else's used pizza?! How do we know it hasn't been poisoned?!"

"No one's touched it, mister. No one other than Mario the pizza maker, that is." The boy stood smiling, arms still fully extended with nothing separating him from the lieutenant's ire but the pizza box.

The lieutenant's eyes narrowed.

"And it's fifty percent off!"

Before the driver had finished pronouncing the final F in *off*, the lieutenant had whipped his wallet out of his back pocket and handed over full payment including a gratuity—a minimal gratuity based on the discounted price.

"Junior, get some paper plates and napkins. Billy, clear the table."

As Pete went to the sideboard to collect the paper goods, Billy barreled past, elbowing him hard in the bicep.

Pete rubbed his arm. The thought of going to the Omni academy became more appealing with each passing moment.

Fearing Billy's version of clearing the table would mean swiping everything onto the floor, Pete quickly removed all of the ceramic plates and put them on the breakfast bar. He'd just lifted the weighty casserole dish and crystal centerpiece when Billy leaned over the table and spread his arms out wide to sweep the surface free of anything his fingers could reach. Salt and pepper shakers, flatware, napkins, and napkin rings all went soaring.

At least nothing broke this time.

"Boys?!" the lieutenant called from the kitchen.

Well-versed in the drill, they ran to their shared bathroom to re-wash their hands for dinner. The brothers jockeyed for position in front of the small sink, and true to form, Billy somehow splashed more water on both their shirtfronts than he did on his hands. He then wiped his palms on his pants and crashed down the hall back to the dining room.

I wonder if kids at the academy have to share sinks.

After four slices of pizza, and what he considered a respectable and unsuspicious interval, Pete placed one last pie wedge on his paper plate. "May I be excused?"

His father, preoccupied with the buttons on his watch, nodded without looking up or speaking.

Pete sped down the hall to his parents' bedroom, desperate to converse with his mother. The pizza was merely a decoy should his father catch him in the act. The years spent perfecting his conflict-avoidance skills had prepared Pete for just this sort of situation.

Cassie lay curled up on her side, softly breathing and peacefully sleeping.

"Mom," he whispered. "Mom!"

She slept on.

"Cassie!"

No change.

"Cassiopeia."

Her eyes snapped open, and she looked at him with an intensity he'd never witnessed in her before, not moving or talking or even blinking.

"Is it true?" he asked, his voice quavering at the prospect of what her answer might import.

She remained still, her eyes locked on his.

"Were you really a great hero like they say? Is there really a school in another dimension?"

"Why are you back in here again, Junior?!" As if on cue, the lieutenant walked in and thwarted the conversation before it could even get going.

His gaze still held by Cassie's, Pete struggled to answer calmly. "I brought some pizza for Mom … I thought she might be hungry when she wakes up."

"Oh. That was thoughtful of you, Junior. Now run along. She needs her rest."

"Yes, sir."

Cassie closed her eyes as Pete left her side, the slightest hint of a smile turning up the corners of her mouth.

"I love you, P.J," she whispered.

"I love you too, Mom."

"I miss you every day," she trailed off.

"Go help your brother clean up the dinner things, Junior. Then brush your teeth and change into your pajamas. We've all had a long day."

Pete returned to the dining room, his heart and steps heavy at the thought Cassie's *I miss you* comment referred to her being routinely opiated and not fully coherent when with her family.

Billy was nowhere in sight, but the ring of pizza crust, pepperoni, and mushroom pieces around the youngest Drake's chair provided evidence he'd once been there. The empty pizza box suggested he wasn't coming back.

Pete tidied up the area and sponged the pizza sauce off Billy's chair, scrubbing vigorously, as if doing so would help reveal some sort of meaning behind his mother's ambiguous reactions—especially her alertness when he called her Cassiopeia and that trace of a smile when she closed her eyes again. Surely, it all must signify something—but what?

The lieutenant sent the boys off to bed early. Billy expressed his opinion on the matter by slamming, opening, and re-slamming doors. Pete didn't mind the premature bedtime, not when there was so much ineffable fodder to ponder. He slipped under the covers and stared up at the sterile ceiling, convinced he'd never be able to fall asleep, not with all the questions racing through his head.

Even so, within minutes, he was deep in slumber, a slight smile like his mother's turning up the corners of his mouth.

His dreams were nearly always the same. They featured a ride in the car with his family or a scene of him in his room, scrawling on his pad of graph paper as he came up with a brilliant idea for an amazing invention that would make the family rich—an idea he could never remember when he awoke the next day.

That night, his dreams brimmed with fantastical imagery. In one scenario, he stood on a small hill looking over a valley that naturally sectioned itself into woods, a lake, a wild-flower-dotted meadow, a short cliff from which fire fell like rain, a manicured park full of topiary animals clad in Victorian fashions, and above it all, a sky like an aurora borealis, its colorful swirls of light fully visible even though it was day.

High up in the sky, approaching each other from opposite quadrants, were a dragon and a Viking ship with a hot air balloon where the sail should be. Pete's lungs burned with the thin, biting air of the upper atmosphere; he was the dragon rider, even as he watched himself from the valley below.

The scene shifted. Heavy wings beat the air on either side of him as he gazed up at a cloudy sky where three hot air balloons rose rapidly, their occupants dressed in apparel suited to a Renaissance Faire. All brandished bladed weapons while hollering at each other. The winged horse that now bore him screeched, its wings frozen. The steed hung mid-air momentarily, then plummeted toward the ground. Pete fell off, crying out in his dream as he fell faster and faster before waking with a jolt, his eyes snapping open as his mother's had.

Instantly alert, his heart raced.

Whoa ...

He went over the dream the best he could, desperate to hold onto it. Fantasy was new territory.

A moment later, he was once again asleep, dreaming of how to mechanize a potato peeler.

CHAPTER EIGHT – A GIFT

{Kapta Ipi}

The next morning, Pete tried to recall his fanciful dream, but was only able to remember the terror and hopelessness he felt when he was falling at the end of it. He shook it off and got out of bed to join his family for breakfast. Clad in his mandated pajamas, robe, and slippers, Pete scuffled out to the dining area to find Lt. Drake preparing the morning meal—not the orange juice, waffles, and strawberries as listed on the monthly menu. No, today the lieutenant was flipping omelettes—a talent Pete had no idea his father possessed.

Pete kept silent as he set the empty table, lest he do or say anything that might disrupt the serenity of the moment. The instant he put a knife and fork in front of Billy, the table pounding began. Cassie was noticeably absent, a fact Pete dared not mention. It was far too controversial, and his father's unusually perky mood merited preservation.

"Hurry up and get dressed for the day, boys. Breakfast will be ready in two shakes."

Pete nodded then sped to his room to change. The moment he returned and took a seat at the table, his father slid a plate in front of him.

Taking a bite of the egg concoction, Pete was pleasantly surprised to find it bursting with flavor—thanks to the inclusion of bacon, cheese, green onions, and tomatoes. "This is really good, Dad," he said, talking with his mouth full, a taboo for which his father normally would have chastised him.

When his mother failed to show after several minutes, Pete racked his brain for a way to inquire about her without risking remonstration. His brother ended up doing the dirty work for him.

"Where's Mom?" Billy blurted, spewing egg fragments in a three-foot radius.

"Your mother is dressing and should be out any second." The lieutenant flipped an omelette high into the air and caught it in the pan held behind his back.

In Pete's estimation, such jocundity did not bode well.

Soon thereafter, Cassie emerged, her habitually sweet and submissive self. "Good morning, boys! Sorry for being such a lay-about. I was having the strangest dream."

Pete scrunched his toes in his shoes to hide his surprise. She never reported having dreams.

"It was about a pirate ship, and this enormous wave rose up behind it, a wave that looked like a woman's face with flowing hair. Then the wave broke over the ship, and the ship was gone. Shall I make some coffee?"

"Sounds like quite the flight of fancy," the lieutenant said, his hands unsteady as he filled a glass with water from the tap and rushed to Cassie's side. "Time for your medication, cupcake."

The rattle of the pills in their bottle sounded like a deadbolt sliding into place, locking his mother back inside her internal prison just as she was starting to saw through its bars.

I need to think ... away from Dad! ... If I go back to the school, maybe I can get some answers from Etta to like my jillion questions!

"Is it okay if I go for a bike ride? I wanna check out the neighborhood before school starts and all."

The milliseconds stretched like taffy as he waited for his father's answer.

"That's a fine idea, Junior."

Victory!

"Some exercise and fresh air will do you good – maybe even make you grow an inch or two."

Pete washed his breakfast dishes with vigor, working quickly to ditch out before his father could change his mind or assign him some menial chore.

"But stay away from that school," the lieutenant added.

Pete halted where he stood. Did his father know about his conversation with Etta? Had his mother mentioned the Omni tidbits he'd tossed out to coax her?

"You already visited the school and still need to get to know the rest of the area. Understood?"

"Yes, sir." Pete grabbed his backpack and hastened to the backyard shed where his bicycle was stored.

He pedaled away with the speed of a time trialist, traveling in the opposite direction of the school. Several streets into his journey, he changed tack and headed straight for the school grounds, keeping an eye out for his father, or worse, Billy.

Pete arrived at the campus to find the doors closed and locked. He circled the perimeter twice searching for Etta, but the site was peopleless and dormant.

She probably doesn't work Sundays.

His plan foiled, he biked away at a crawl, going nowhere in particular.

A small park caught his attention. Just like the day before, the colors of the flora and sky burst with vibrancy. Ducks preened on a tiny pond, and a pair of squirrels raced around in a sort of tumultuous competition to hoard the most acorns. Pete pulled up to the park's solitary willow, a sprawling tree with boughs that appeared to dance a choreographed cha-cha despite the lack of detectable breeze.

Now this *is a good spot for thinking ... or maybe even some design brainstorming.*

After selecting the perfect patch of grass to sit on, he opened his backpack, intending to take out his drawing supplies and launch into some concerted inventing. Only, for once he wasn't in the mood. Instead, he zipped his backpack closed and leaned against the tree to revel in the scenery. It wasn't long before he gave in to the temptation to shut his eyes and forget about everything—his inventions, his parents, his new school, even the intriguing academy.

A shadow blocked the sun's warmth, sending a quick shiver from head to toe. Opening his eyes, he was startled to find a grizzled man standing over him holding a rake, wearing a conical nón lá hat and clothing that appeared more apropos to karate than gardening.

"Mornin'!" the man said, tipping his hat back to reveal a heavily lined and pallid visage. "I wake you?"

Pete blinked and scrambled to stand.

"Now don't be gettin' up on my account. Didn't mean to disturb."

So much for serenity.

Unsure what to say, Pete nodded at the man's outfit. "Are you the gardener here?"

The man stood the rake on its end and adjusted his hat's stampede string. "Why, yes, Guardener for this whole region. Lots to guard in these parts."

Pete's fingertips tingled. *What does "lots to guard" mean? ... Is this guy someone like Etta?*

The fact the rake remained standing upright after the man let go of it should have tipped Pete off that this man was *different*.

Pete leaned in and whispered. "Do you know about Omni?"

"You know, the word *omni* means all. I don't know all."

Drat.

The man struggled to bend and lower his body so that he might sit. "But yes, I be knowin' 'bout Omni."

Yes!

Pete sat back down.

"We Guardeners be charged with protectin' our regions from outside threats and all, especially prospective students."

"Prospective students are threats?"

The man chuckled. "Nooooo, that's who we be protectin' … from outside threats like the XQ rebels or Sun Zellies."

Rebels? What rebels? Who's rebelling ... and against who ... and where ... and why?!

"What was that about rebels?"

"Etta done mentioned she was in the way of meetin' you. Fine woman, Etta."

"Is Etta a guardian—"

"Guardener."

"Is she one too?"

The man removed his hat, uncovering a shiny jet-black braid rolled into a circle on the crown of his head. "She be a Custodian. She and her like be seein' to the day's needs of them under their care. We Guardeners be the sentries who be in the way of decidin' who's and what's allowed into our regions. Once we done let someone in, it be up to the Custodians to be lookin' after 'em."

"Sounds reasonable."

The man paused before speaking again. "Etta done said you be knowin' not a jot about t'Ocademy or t'Omniverse … That true?"

"Yesterday was the first I'd ever heard about any of it. Was my mom really some kind of famous hero person?"

"Your mama was done like no one else—and scarabs but she could hold her own—the combo-na-shi-on of a brave protector, wise leader, loyal friend, and compassionate stranger."

"Was she like a Florence Nightingale or something?"

The man choked. "Nightingale! Don't be lettin' your mama done hear none of that Nitrin talk! Not if you don't want her to done have a relapse! 'Twas heartbreakin' what done happened to her. She be lucky she bein' alive. If she'd not done come out of that long night—"

"Long night?"

"That weeks-on-end sleep. If she'd not done come out of it, she would never done had progenies, and we two wouldn't be jawin' right now."

Pete's pancreas pulsed at the profundity of the man's words. The event that nearly cost his mother her life was an off-limits subject—one on which he'd never been able to get a straight answer. "I'm not really sure what happened to my mom exactly. Do you know?"

The man looked up at the sky, then back at Pete. "Name be Leon, by the bayou."

"Nice to meet you, Leon. I'm—"

"Oh, I know who you be, Peyton. I've been knowin' for nigh on fourteen years, five months, three weeks, six days, and a tinch over an hour, more or less."

Pete's lips formed an unnatural pursed grin as he strove to conceal his surprise.

"Now 'bout your mama and her sit-u-a-shi-on. The story could be takin' many a day to be tellin', but we be havin' no time for that right now."

Pete's odd grin drooped.

"Not to be discouraged, young Drake. You'll be havin' plenty o' time to learn about ta great Cassiopeia. There be tributes to her posted all over her estate."

"Estate? Umm, we live in military housing."

Leon disregarded the comment. "For now, let me just be sayin', if your mama twere anyone else, she'd be six feet down pushin' up the wildflowers."

Pete let out a sigh he'd been holding for years. "I always suspected Mom's strong medication was to blame for the way she was. It never occurred to me that she could've stayed in a coma … or even died."

"No one at t'hospital done expected her t'ever wake up. No one but your papa, that is. Every day after he done finished work and school, there he be at her bedside, bringing her flowers, reading to her, rubbing life back into her limbs, singing to her."

"My dad sings?!"

"He surely done used to. I don't know about nowadays. I tell you, I'm of a mind that it was his ministrations saw Cassiopeia through and brought her back from t'other side. Once she done woke, they done married. Soon beyond that they done welcomed you and your youngin' brother into t'Omniverse."

"Billy! I didn't even think of him. Will he be going to the academy too?"

"Uh, no."

Pete's grin resurrected.

"As for your mama's tremors a few years back …" Leon adjusted his sitting position and cleared his throat. "Her system was done weakened by her earlier injuries and coma, you could say. So when a piece of grievous news done triggered her, she done short-circuited and seized up somethin' terrible. Your papa and the doctors feared she'd done go comatose again, so they took steps to keep her right … But that all be in the past now. Today she be fit as a Dim Phi fiddle, and you and I be here jawin'. Which brings us to *why* we be jawin'. So how 'bout let's get down to steel farthin's."

Pete's neck tensed up, and he squeezed his hands together to help him concentrate. "I don't know what half of what you said means, but I'm listening."

The man smiled. "If more of us done listened, imagine what a peaceful world it would be! I can see why Omni be needin' you."

"How could a school *need* me?"

Leon shook his head and chuckled. "I done keep forgettin' how nescient you be about t'Omniverse. You haven't done just been accepted into t'Ocademy this time … You've done been pressganged!"

"What do you mean *this time*?"

"Your papa's done ignored every Ocademy acceptance letter and request messengered since you done turned ten."

"Did you say since I was *ten*?!"

"Yessirree. Ocademy students be rangin' in age from ten, eleven t' twenty, twenty-one. Most recruits be enterin' as first-level conscripts, but you'll be arrivin' at the fourth-level, so you'll be havin' a passel o' catchin' up to be doin'."

Pete hung his head. "I can't. I'm really sorry."

"Just be doin' your best, young Drake. No one be expectin' you t' learn t'all of it at one go."

"No, Mr. Leon, what I mean is I can't go to the academy."

"Surely you can! Your mama done did. And your papa done woulda if he done coulda."

Pete's pancreas twisted while his mind juggled Leon's words as if they were patients at an emergency ward on a holiday weekend. Pete kept coming back to just one part—the part about him being needed.

I've never felt needed *before.*

"… So if I was thinking of maybe paying a visit to the academy … just to check it out. Ya know, out of curiosity to see where my mom went to school and all …"

Leon held out a copy of the Omni recruitment letter. "Then you'd be needin' this and needin' it inscribed."

Pete merely stared at the document, as if touching it would somehow seal his fate.

"Son, in this life, I've done found it be our choices that be definin' us, not our circumstances. You've done been presented with a choice. A choice be a gift. What will you be doin' with this gift?"

After several seconds of the paper quivering in Leon's unsteady hand, Pete gently took it and slid it into the front pouch of his backpack, saying nothing.

Leon lifted Pete's chin with a gnarled forefinger and looked warmly into his eyes. "Your answer, son."

Maybe I could go for a couple of days and tell Dad the academy people kidnapped me, and that I made a death-defying escape to come back home.

Pete slowly nodded. "Yes." His mouth had not consulted his mind before answering, and he trapped his upper lip with his teeth to avoid further infractions. He was far too rational to seriously consider whisking off to some mythical place he'd only heard of the day before. Being at a new school at a new base was bad enough.

Then again, Leon said I was needed—actually needed.

Leon turned away with a weary smile, commenting to parties unseen. "He be comin'. Best inform Esperança." Turning back, Leon put a hand on Pete's shoulder. "Your letter needs inscribin' in the most imperative way or you done won't be goin'. Understood? … And don't be harborin' any foolish notions about forgin' the inscription. Can always smell a forgery, and forgers be banned from t'Ocademy, for life! Get it signed proper. We all be countin' on you, Peyton Jayce Drake."

No one had ever counted on him for anything. But the people from the other-worldly school where his mother had been a hero needed him and were counting on him. Gallantry got the better of him before good sense had a chance to rein him in. "I'll get it signed, Mr. Leon. I don't know how, but I will!"

Leon grinned. "Good lad! That's what I done been wantin' to hear. Lookee then, Etta and I be meetin' you right under this tree at six o'clock brisk tomorrow mornin'. *This* be your departure spot. Clear?"

"You mean this exact spot? Whoa. What a lucky coincidence I sat here."

Leon leaned forward with an impish smirk. "Be it a coincidence?" Stiffly, he rose and steadied himself on his rocky feet. "You mind?" he asked, pointing to his hat.

Pete stood and handed the nón lá to him, failing to register that the rake was inching toward the Guardener. "You okay, Mr. Leon?"

"Better than ever." Leon smiled broadly and pulled the hat down snugly over his braid roll. He then resumed raking, working his way around the tree while whistling a melody Pete had heard his mother hum now and again.

Fueled by an energy that was foreign to him, Pete got on his bike and slid his arms through the straps of his backpack. "See you in the morning, Mr. Leon!"

As he pedaled toward home in a cloud of exhilaration and newfound purpose, an uncomfortable thought began to needle him, rendering his bike seat nearly unbearable to sit on. Each rotation of his bicycle's chain was a link of disjointed information falling into place.

He'd long suspected the troubles at home had started on his tenth birthday. By all accounts, that was the day he would've received his first academy acceptance letter. It was also the day his parents got into the argument to end all arguments—the one that led to Cassie's massive seizure.

Pete never learned the source of their row, but he'd always sensed it had something to do with *the girl in white* who came to the door saying she had some sort of telegram for his mother and a delivery for him—a delivery he never received. The girl in white's visit ignited a quarrel so heated that instead of his parents watching Pete open birthday presents, they shut themselves in their bedroom to discuss *custody arrangements.*

The cardboard walls had provided nothing in the way of privacy, and Pete listened intently as his parents agreed that Cassie would move out with Pete; the lieutenant would stay on the base with Billy. When the time came for Pete to blow out the ten-shaped candle on his cake, his wish had been simple: *Please keep my family together.*

The hours-long clash came to a stop when Cassie collapsed and fell into a fit. The remainder of Pete's birthday was spent at the hospital.

He did get his birthday wish—his family stayed together, although in slightly fractured form. The lieutenant turned hyper-protective. Cassie began taking mind-numbing medication. Billy became a brute. During the intervening years, the family dynamic steadily deteriorated, and Pete became increasingly desperate to restore the happiness of his single-digit years.

I wish I could go back in time and intercept the girl in white before she got to the house. Someday I'll invent a time machine and fix everything!

He was nearly to the corner leading to the new bungalow when he made a turn to extend his ride—he needed more time to think. For as long as he could remember, Pete believed the problems at home were his fault. His parent's big fight had been about him, and they still occasionally squabbled about matters concerning him, primarily when Cassie's medication started to wear off. If he were to leave, maybe his father wouldn't be a neurotic tyrant, maybe his mother wouldn't be a convivial zombie, and maybe his younger brother wouldn't be l'enfant terrible.

Leon said a choice is a gift. I'm gonna use this gift to make my family happy again. My choice is to go to the academy.

Clamping his mouth shut to avoid swallowing a bug flying straight at him, his tongue moved across the sore spot on his upper lip where he'd bitten it after saying yes to Leon.

I guess my mouth knew my answer before my brain did.

He steered his bike homeward, finding peace in his radical decision to attend the academy, despite the fact the decision presented immense change. On moving day, his mother had waxed nostalgically about her school days. Maybe Pete's experience at the academy would be just as pleasant and strife-free.

The closer he got to the bungalow, the more his palms sweat.

How the heck am I going to get a parent signature by tomorrow morning? If I ask Mom to sign it, she'll just say, "Of course, P.J. As long as your dad says it's all right." He's gonna find out. He always does! ... Maybe I could rig some sort of doodad that would make him sign it in his sleep. Or maybe I could slip him one of Mom's pills so he doesn't realize what he's signing ...

Who am I kidding? This is gonna be a disaster. I may very well set off World War III.

CHAPTER NINE – SEEKING APPROVAL

{Kapta Oneu}

Pete's nerve-racked palms slid off the bungalow's back door knob more than once. He found his father sitting alone in the living room reading a biography of someone Pete assumed was a famous Marine or football player. Billy was out *playing*, as his father put it. Cassie was again resting.

Carpe diem ... no time like the present ... now or never ... I'm gonna regret this.

"Dad, can I talk to you?"

The lieutenant didn't bother taking his eyes off his book. "What is it, Junior?"

"It's about school."

"Nothing to worry about. Your grades are fine, and no one will notice you. They never do."

They do now!

"Umm ... well ... there's another school I wanna go to."

His father looked up, his jaw taut. "No son of mine is going to some hoity-toity private school! Public education made me the man I am today."

That's not much of a selling point for public school!

"I'm not really sure what the place is," Pete said. "All I know is they really want me to go."

Lt. Drake closed his book and turned his full attention to his son.

Being the object of his father's spotlight instantly drained Pete of his high-octane post-park energy. Pete's nearly numb fingers haltingly unzipped the pouch of his backpack and produced the recruitment letter.

As his father scanned the page, his complexion cycled from tanned bronze to bruised purple to deathly ash and back to bronze in a matter of seconds. "Where did you get this?" he asked, his tone terrifyingly controlled.

Bile rising in Pete's throat and threatening to escape his mouth, he blurted, "A man raking leaves at the park gave it to me."

The lieutenant slammed back in his chair. "They already found you," he whispered to himself. His darting eyes stretched so wide the crimson of his inner lids shown.

Pete clenched the backpack hard to prevent picking at his thumbs, keeping his tone measured and doing his best to discuss the subject in a way that would not send his father into a cataclysmic tirade. "He said they need me and that I'm scheduled to leave tomorrow."

His father said nothing, his expression unreadable.

So it's not a no. This is good!

"The man also said something about Mom being a legendary hero … I figured you'd want me to go to school there too, out of respect for Mom and all."

Playing the mom card's sure to seal the deal!

The lieutenant grabbed Pete's arm rigidly and spoke calmly. "You have nothing to worry about, Junior. You hear me? You're safe. I'm going to take care of everything." Lt. Drake pulled Pete into a rare embrace. His breath was erratic as he squeezed Pete uncomfortably tight.

I've never seen Dad scared before.

"You're my son, Junior. It's my job to protect you."

Now I'm scared too!

The lieutenant inhaled sharply and pulled his shoulders back. Stepping away from Pete, he tore the Omni letter into as many pieces as he could and placed them on the coffee table. After dumping the contents of a metal trashcan onto the floor, he dropped the ripped-up paper bits into it. He then hastened to the kitchen and took a box of matches off the windowsill, set the receptacle on the floor, lit a match, and released it into the can.

Pete let out an imperceptible whimper as he watched his plan to save his family go up in smoke.

His father's complexion returned to normal once the document had been fully incinerated. "Did you lock up your bike?" he asked softly. "… Junior … Junior!"

"Huh?"

"I asked you if you locked your bike."

Pete heard only part of the question. "Bike?"

The lieutenant clapped his hands in front of Pete's face. "Focus, Junior."

Pete jumped. "My bike? No, not yet. Sorry, sir. I'll do it right now." He turned to go to the backyard, but his father put an arm out to block him.

"Never mind, son. I'll do it."

"I'm really sorry, Dad. It won't happen again."

His father took him by the elbow and ushered him to his bedroom.

"Ow, Dad, that hurts."

"It's for your own good, son."

"But I haven't done anything!"

"Nor will you. I'll make sure of it." He held Pete by the shoulders and pushed him down into a sitting position on the bed. "Cupcake," he hollered, "can you come in here? I need your help."

A moment later, Cassie entered the room, her eyes bleary as though she'd just awakened.

"Make sure Junior stays put. Don't let him out of this room … and don't let anyone in!"

She nodded. The lieutenant rushed out. Pete gawped.

"What's going on?" Cassie asked with a hint of a slur. The increased dosage of medication the lieutenant had administered made her groggier than usual.

"I have no clue. Seriously, I didn't do anything."

Pete's pancreas chewed on his emotions to gauge if he felt more indignant or confused or worried. He definitely felt all three.

The grating metal of what sounded like an electric saw came from the backyard, and in a flash, gory scenes from every horror movie Pete had ever seen bombarded his brain.

Okay, now I'm mostly worried.

His mother sat on the bed next to him and put her hand on his back, rubbing it gently as he chewed his thumb cuticles.

"Why does he hate me so much?" Pete asked.

"Hate you?! Just the opposite! The sacrifices he's made to protect you …"

"Protect me! From what? Life? Just because he's a Marine doesn't mean I have to live in a bomb shelter! It's not fair. He's not like this with Billy!"

"No, he's not. But that's because Billy is … well he's not …"

"Not what?"

"Not you, for starters."

"Like I said, he hates me."

The lieutenant rushed back into the room carrying a selection of boards under one arm, a hefty cordless drill in his opposing hand, and several long nails poking out of his mouth. He walked straight to the window and shoved back its curtains. A departure from his normal systematic approach to projects, he attached the boards to the window's frame at random, glancing at his watch every few seconds and stopping at the slightest sound.

Pete attempted to employ his usual coping technique of imagining his father wearing a wacky getup. Instead, his mind strobed with the picture of his father wearing a welder's mask and hoisting a blood-tipped chainsaw.

Within minutes, an unruly mass of wood covered the glass, obstructing all sunlight.

Beyond worried.

Holding the drill like a gun, the lieutenant turned to Pete. "Do you need to use the toilet?"

"Do I what? No, but—"

"Good. Then stay here … and don't move!" He hurried over to the bedroom door and removed the doorknob, his brow perspiring. He then re-attached the knob and fiddled with it for several seconds. "There. The lock is on the outside now, and I've blocked the knob's escape pinhole. If someone manages to get in, they won't be able to get out."

The severity of the situation emboldened Pete to speak out. "But what if *I* need to get out? Like if there's a fire or something?"

"Just call out, and I'll come running. You can count on it, Junior!"

"I don't understand. Why am I being punished? … If it's about my bike—"

Cassie gave his hand a gentle squeeze. "*Shhhhh*. You need to trust your dad, P.J. He knows what's best … for all of us."

"Junior, you are to stay in this room until it's time to go to school, *this* town's school two days from now. Your mother will bring you your meals, and I will escort you to the head to use the toilet and brush your teeth. You can shower Tuesday morning before going to class. Is that clear?"

His internal processor shorting out, Pete nodded perfunctorily.

"Cassie, come with me." The lieutenant held the door open for his wife then exited behind her and shut Pete in. "Open the door, Junior," he called from the hallway.

"What? But—" Pete put his hand on the knob and tried to turn it. "It's not working."

"It's working just fine from where I stand." A moment later, his father burst back into the room.

"Dad, I'm really sorry—for whatever I did."

"Where's your backpack?"

Pete nodded toward his chair.

"You won't need it 'til Tuesday. Can't take any chances." The lieutenant grabbed the bag and again exited and locked the door, trapping Pete in the sunless room and leaving him with nothing to do but churn in resentment and dream of running away from home.

CHAPTER TEN – DOUBLE CHOCOLATE INJUSTICE

{Kapta Anenn}

Pete sat on his bed in the gloom, the room's only illumination coming from beneath the locked door. He could've easily flipped the overhead light switch on, but opted for the dark, embracing the bleakness of his predicament. He'd expected some sort of *issue* with his father over the academy letter, but his current level of incarceration without explanation was a concept beyond his grasp. His chance to go to the academy had been snatched away without his getting a vote—just when he'd warmed to the idea and told Leon he could count on him.

I wish I'd never even heard of the academy. I wish we'd never moved to this stupid town!

He fell back flat on his bed, his thoughts landing on arbitrary and trivial topics. Had his father put his bike back in the shed? What would his mom be making for dinner? Did Sally Daniels return his favorite pen she borrowed in class last week? Did that rake at the park move by itself? Where was the academy located? Did kids in this new town talk with an accent? What bedlam was Billy instigating during all of this? Was his father really going to keep him locked up all weekend? Were Etta and Leon even real?

The unfamiliar sensation of warmth trickling down his face informed him tears were leaking out of his eyes. He never cried. Not that he had a problem with crying. It just wasn't an activity for which he had much use. Avoiding social interaction and conflict went hand-in-hand with avoiding crying.

The more his tears fell, the more his angst grew.

Despite the coolness of the room, bubbles of perspiration collected on his upper lip. The air felt stifling and sour. He unleashed his frustration by yanking on the boards across the windows. His raw cuticles bled. The boards remained intact. He collapsed onto his bony bed and in the absence of more tears, merely gurgled and rocked.

I can't do this. I'm no hero like Etta said Mom was, or like Superman or Batman or whoever everyone at school wants to be. I don't even wanna to be a hero. I just wanna ... be.

A low growl from his stomach reminded him he hadn't had lunch. Despite his hunger, the thought of food turned his stomach. He felt discomfort that extended beyond his pancreas and cuticles to parts of his psyche he couldn't identify.

It's all so unfair.

Raised voices came from his parents' bedroom. Their tone suggested Pete's situation had not gone over well with his mother, and he feared the upshot would lead to yet more medication for her and stricter treatment for himself.

I've gotta get out of here. That's all there is to it.

* * *

He wasn't aware he'd fallen asleep until a quiet rapping on the door wakened him.

"P.J., may I come in?"

"Sure, Mom," he droned.

She opened the door and stood in the doorway, a lunch tray balanced on one palm. To Pete, her dark figure juxtaposed against the brilliance of the natural light pouring in behind her made her look like a firefighter charging into a room to make a rescue as savage flames licked her back.

Maybe she's come to save me. After all, she's supposedly a hero!

He raised his head. "Are you here to let me out?"

"You know I can't do that, P.J."

He dropped his head back on the pillow. "I'm not hungry."

"That's all right." From behind her back she produced a jumbo glass of frothy joy. "More double-chocolate-cookie milkshake for me."

He sat up to regard her, willing himself to view her as a person, not just a mother. A pang of empathy washed over him, overtaking his desire to wallow. After all she'd been through—whatever it had been—he didn't have the heart to put her through more. He knew his situation with his dad was a strain on her as well. The least he could do was accept the treat she'd made for him.

He affected a smile and put his hand out to take the glass. "Then again, I'm a growing boy and need to keep up my strength."

The cool cream of the milkshake soothed the acid in his throat as his mother's gentle presence soothed his soul. She always knew exactly what to do to make everything better.

Their pleasant interlude turned out to be short-lived. The lieutenant entered moments later, instructing Cassie to keep the door locked and grumbling something about safety and coddling.

Pete was once more left alone in the dark, feeling anything but safe or coddled—more like railroaded and unjustly jailed.

I'll just have to wait and not do anything to make him mad so that he lets me out. He can't keep me in here forever ... Who am I kidding? He's never letting me out.

Little by little, he noshed on the lunch items his mother delivered, eating to satiate boredom more than hunger. Once the food disappeared, so did his patience with the darkness.

He trudged over to the light switch and flipped it. The stark brightness caused him to clamp his eyes closed, plunging him back into momentary blackness. When his sight normalized, he looked around the room and found it even drearier than it seemed in the dark.

The same went for his circumstances. The milkshake threatened to come back up at the thought he'd be disappointing Leon and Etta who would be waiting under a tree at the crack of dawn for a kid locked in his room.

Desperate to find something, anything, that would take his mind off his plight, he ransacked his desk drawers. The contents amounted to a wooden ruler along with a cigar box containing baseball cards, a few paperclips, some bubble gum, a couple of marbles, and a pen—not the pen he'd lent Sally Daniels.

He considered reading, but was too wound up to do so. Besides, his books were still boxed up with the family photo albums in the garage.

What I really need is some foxhole combat ... That's it!

He dove into his closet to hunt for his little green army, confident synthetic warfare would mollify his crushed spirits and frayed nerves. Despite the fewness of his possessions, he was unable to locate the box that held his fort and soldiers.

This is ridiculous. Where could two entire regiments have gone?

It was then he recalled Billy-the-bully had swiped the box the day they moved in. At the time, wishing to avoid an altercation—especially one that would result in bruises—Pete had let the affront slide. He knew Billy wanted to get a rise out of him, and Pete had been determined not to grant him the pleasure. Pete planned to fetch the box after the novelty of the theft had worn off for Billy, but forgot about it until that moment.

For the first time in as long as he could remember, Pete regretted not standing up to Billy. If he'd handled the situation with his brother differently, he'd have his army with him now, and maybe, just maybe, Billy would learn to be nice, or at least, less annoying.

Mom said she had a bully in school when she was young who turned into a friend. Why didn't I ever ask how she did it?

Facing his failures made Pete feel two-dimensional and hollow. His time alone in his room had sent him through a ropes course of emotions that exhausted him body and soul.

I've had it!

He flung his stuff back into the closet with force—too indignant to bother being careful. When he hurled his laundry bag, a sort of rustling noise caught his attention. He rifled through the clothing, searching for what he assumed must be a dry leaf, until he came to the shirt he'd worn the day before when he walked to the new school.

In that instant, he remembered Etta had placed a copy of his recruitment letter in his shirt pocket. Breathlessly, he reached inside the pocket and retrieved the paper, unfolding it as if he were handling butterfly wings.

The letter was his mulligan. He knew it and meant to make the most of it. "Thank you for the second chance, Etta. I won't waste it," he whispered.

He stood immobile for a moment, considering where to conceal the parchment. Ultimately, he slid it into the back of his pillowcase. It was the best he could come up with on the spot.

All was not lost after all. He only needed to get his mother's signature and get out of his inescapable prison—and make pigs fly.

CHAPTER ELEVEN – WITHOUT A NET

{Kapta Anenn-An}

Pete walked in circles to get his mind in motion. All it accomplished was making him dizzy.

Finding a backup academy letter was the last thing he expected. He stared at the pillowcase where he'd hidden the document, his spartan room a stark reminder that he would be walking his tightrope to freedom without a safety net—more specifically, without the benefit of his sketchpad, his official 0.9 inventing pencil, or his T-square, all of which were in his confiscated backpack. He tried writing on his hand with the lone pen from his desk. It was out of ink. He shut the drawer with a huff, cursing Sally Daniels for taking his best pen.

In the absence of his cassette player, he turned on the television for background noise.

It took all of three minutes for his father to catch wind of the activity and put a stop to it. "Have you lost your mind, Junior? A blaring television could attract attention!" Without further comment, he removed the television from the room.

A moment later, the lieutenant returned, flipped Pete's light off, and locked the door again as he exited.

Pete was unfazed—past the point of being disturbed by his father's actions. The more the lieutenant took away, the more Pete resolved to *get* away. After all, he would be doing it for the good of the family, since he believed most of the turmoil at home revolved around him. Plus, he was needed.

He resumed walking in circles, this time going the other way as he began mentally outlining his objectives. More than once he nearly tripped over the long cable his father had detached from the television.

First, I have to get Mom's signature – even if I have to put a pen in her hand and guide it over the paper myself!

As for breaking out of his confinement, he'd need to find a means of getting the door open—no way could he remove the layers of thick boards blocking the window. If only he had some sort of door-unlocking apparatus. His father had jammed shut the pinhole on the doorknob inside the room—the hole designed to allow for emergency escapes—so that option was out.

Pete was accustomed to making ridiculous, elaborate devices designed to do basic tasks. This was different. In fact, it was the opposite. He needed to create something simple that would go undetected while being highly effective. And he needed to do it fast.

The prospect sent a surge of invigorating adrenaline through his system. He felt his face warm and shoulders relax.

Getting out of a locked room? No sweat ... Well, maybe a little sweat.

Again he paced, and again he nearly tripped over the annoying cable that served as a reminder of his father's inexplicable punishment. As he knelt and rolled the cable to store it out of the way, an escape plan popped into his head. The plan was <u>fully formed</u> and possibly doable—and the key was in his hands.

It was a risky scheme with multiple steps and specific procedures that would have to be executed flawlessly. Both the project and the idea of liberation simultaneously galvanized and terrified him. Drumming his fingers on his thigh, he thought through a checklist of what he would need based on what he could easily lay hold of. Mercifully, there were only a few items required: a paperclip, a piece of bubble gum, a ruler, some dental floss, and most important, the pesky television cable.

The only thing missing from the room was the floss, but he'd be able to grab that from the bathroom when he went to brush his teeth just before turning in. He hastened to his desk drawer to retrieve all three paperclips and one piece of the gum, putting them in his pocket so they would be at the ready when it was time to make his prison break.

Foremost was his need to procure his mother's signature, or all his plotting would be for naught. Even more stressful, he'd have to wait until she came back to the room.

I can't call down the hall for her cuz the door's locked. And if I pound on the door, you can bet Dad will be the one who will open it! No, I'm gonna have to be patient ... Looks like we're back to pigs flying.

To pass the time, he returned to bed and reclined, daydreaming of what life at the academy might be like. Were the other dimensions similar to his? Would the school be located on another planet, or would it be somewhere right under everyone's nose like in the Statue of Liberty's crown? Would he meet strange creatures he'd never heard of? Would he meet strange creatures he *had* heard of? His toes wiggled at the thought he might actually meet a dragon.

Dragons!

Soon, a faint rapping on the door told Pete his mother had returned.

"Come in, Mom."

She entered looking weary, like someone coming off a chain gang, their spirit broken—a far cry from a hero. "Your father asked me to tell you that you can go for a walk with him before dinner if you'd like. There's one thing though ...You'll have to ... well, you'll have to be on a leash."

"A what?!" Pete squawked.

"He says it's to ensure your safety, P.J."

"Pass." He lay back down, his resolve to flee skyrocketing.

A moment of static silence passed between them. Cassie closed the door and sat on the edge of his bed.

Time to make my move.

"Mom, will you do something for me – no matter how hard it might be?"

"Of course, P.J. You know I will."

Pete sat up again and studied her, trying to gauge if she was up to the challenge of flouting the lieutenant's commands. "I don't know what you remember about the Academy of Omnisopol … Omniphoscent … the Omni academy, but I got a letter from them. They want me to go to school there. And I thought as long as I have to start a new school, maybe I should start it there … since you went there and all."

She scratched the side of her neck as her gaze danced across the ceiling. "Sorry, where?"

He slipped the academy letter out of his pillowcase and carefully handed it to her. "I need you to sign this, Mom. Please."

"What is it, sweetheart?" Upon reading the document, her eye twitched, and her fingers waggled as if she were laboring to work out a concept just beyond her grasp. Her breath caught. "Edisyuh id Deora!" She whipped her head in the direction of the closed door, then grabbed Pete's shoulders and looked into his eyes with the same intensity she'd shown the night before. "P.J. you must get rid of that, right away. If your father were to … You can't begin to fathom … It could tear this family apart."

"That's why I'm coming to you. I need *your* signature, Mom. It's the only way."

She shook her head vehemently and thrust the letter back into his hand. "P.J., I can't. You don't know what you're asking. I'm sorry, but I just can't!" She nearly lost her balance as she got to her feet and hurried toward the door.

"You won't tell Dad, will you?" Pete begged.

Wordlessly, she exited and locked the door.

It was several seconds before her footsteps receded. He returned the letter to his pillowcase and picked at his cuticles, his pancreas pinching in *I told you so* smugness.

As long as she doesn't tell him about the letter, I should be okay. Please don't tell him ... pleaaaaaaase!

Voraciously he chewed his thumbs, unable to focus on anything but his fear over what his father might do.

After several excruciatingly suspenseful minutes, his father opened the door.

Pete sat on his hands to hide his torn-up thumbs.

The lieutenant blocked the doorway, staring at Pete stone-faced for seconds on end.

She did it. I can't believe she did it. She ratted me out to Dad.

As the lieutenant approached the bed, Pete instinctively scooted back, praying the paper secreted in his pillowcase wouldn't rustle and give away its existence.

The lieutenant wandered the room, looking over Pete's things. "I hear you declined my offer to go for a walk."

Pete sat silent and stationary, unsure how to answer.

"I'm betting you could use a toilet break by now."

"Yes, sir."

"All right. Run along then."

Pete couldn't tell if this was some sort of trick to get him out of the room so his father could search it, but as his bladder was nearly bursting and he didn't know when he'd be allowed a restroom break again, he dashed across the hall.

"Leave the door open."

Pete grimaced at the indignity, but resisted commenting. No sense rocking the boat. While in the bathroom, he considered making a grab for the dental floss, then decided not to take the chance with the door open. No, the floss would have to wait until tooth-brushing time just before bed.

He returned to his room to find the lieutenant in the midst of a second search of the desk drawers.

"What did I tell you about chewing this stuff? It'll rot your teeth!" Grumbling in disapproval, his father pocketed the pack of gum as well as the inkless pen and box of baseball cards.

Pete let out an imperceptible *whew,* thankful he'd already stowed a piece of gum and the paper clips in his pocket. "Are you really going to keep me locked up in here 'til Tuesday morning?"

The lieutenant shot him a long look that Pete was unable to read. Pete was not in the habit of being so direct with his father, but then again, he'd never been on the verge of going to another dimension and maybe meeting a dragon.

The lieutenant resumed patrolling, bending down to peer into the floor heater, looking inside Pete's closet. "Not necessarily. You'll be free to go right after those menaces from Omni leave the area. Simply tell me the time they instructed you to rendezvous. Half-an-hour after that is when I'll let you out."

Pete chewed the inside of his cheek. As much relied on his answer as it did on his mother's signature. He opted for deceit. "They said, 'When the sun is at its highest.' I guess that means noon?"

His father exhaled and steadied himself against the doorframe. "Yes, son, you're right. That's when the sun is at its highest—twelve hundred hours tomorrow. Then it will all be over." He made a start to program his watch, but his fingers kept fumbling. Instead, he placed his hands behind his back and cleared his throat. "At twelve-thirty, you and Billy can help me rake up the leaves in the front yard. I'll ask your mom to bake you boys a back-to-school cake. How does that sound?"

It was the mention of the rake rather than the cake that made an impression on Pete. He'd vowed to meet rake-man Leon at 6 a.m.

My plan has to work—it just has to!

"Cheer up, Junior. In nineteen hours, this nightmare will finally be behind us. Then you can really enjoy your last day before school starts." The lieutenant sauntered out the door and closed it, jiggling the locked knob.

"*Thirteen* hours, more like it," Pete said under his breath, calculating the time until his unauthorized departure.

Alone again, he wrestled with the question of when to initiate his flight sequence. If he left too early and his father realized he was gone, it would give the lieutenant enough time to pursue him and drag him home. If Pete cut it too close and something went wrong, he could miss his rendezvous. Not to mention there was still the matter of getting his mother's signed approval.

He'd have one last chance to persuade her, and that chance would be in less than an hour.

CHAPTER TWELVE – POT ROAST & PAPER CLIPS

{Kapta Anenn-Be}

The heady aroma of homey food wafted into the room as Cassie cracked open the bedroom door and entered. "Who's in the mood for pot roast?" she asked in a cheery tone, her hands cradling a bountiful dinner plate, her eyes cast down.

"It smells great. Thanks," Pete said mechanically, taking the plate from her and setting it on his desk. Softly, he closed the door. This would be his final opportunity to get her signature. He was all too aware what was at stake. He was also aware there were a million things that could go wrong.

"Mom, I have a plan for how to make things better around here at home – the way they used to be, when I was little, before … Anyway, I can't do it without you."

She lifted her sorrow-filled eyes to meet his gaze.

He then walked over to the bed to produce the letter again. "Please, Mom. Just sign it … It's the right thing to do."

She looked away and heaved a mournful sigh, then turned to leave.

He grabbed at her arm to keep her from going, but she pulled away and darted out, sobbing as she pulled the door closed.

Stunned, Pete dropped onto the bed and stared at the unsigned paper.

I just had to push it. I just had to add that last part, "It's the right thing to do." What was I thinking?! I blew it. I totally blew it.

Again, he lost his appetite. He also lost his second chance. His desolate existence at a humdrum school with a stifling homelife in a nondescript house with two bullies would have to suffice, and he mocked himself for daring to believe he could fix his family, let alone possibly meet a dragon.

Cassie burst back into the room brandishing a Bic ballpoint. She snatched the paper out of his hand, signed it, tucked it down the front of his shirt, hid the pen up her sleeve, crushed him in a hug, whispered the words, "Cheriste som," and once more darted from the room, wiping her eyes as she closed and locked the door.

Pete stood unmoving, not yet absorbing what just happened. Slowly, he withdrew the document from underneath his shirt, watching the door as he did so. After confirming the signature was legible, he stashed the paper back in his pillowcase.

His joy and appetite returned together, and he gobbled up the pot roast and potatoes, relishing the meal as a victory feast. He couldn't help chuckling as he ate, pondering how quickly defeat can turn to success, and vice versa. His eyes kept checking the clock, reinforcing the possibility his whole life might turn topsy-turvy in less than twelve hours.

After lapping up every morsel on his plate, he got into bed in an effort to sleep. He realized it would be his only opportunity to do so, as he planned to stay awake from the time he brushed his teeth until he made his early morning getaway.

He wished to leave a hard-hitting, melodramatic goodbye note. He also wished he had something with which to compose it. But since his father had stripped him of all writing supplies, he'd have to telephone his parents once he arrived, or beam them a message, or make contact in whatever way one did at an interdimensional school.

* * *

Pete remained in a semi-lucid state, too alert to fully surrender to sleep, despite his desire to dream about dragons again. Even so, he was startled when his father entered the room at nine thirty.

"Wake up, Junior. You don't want to be up all night, do you?"

Actually, I pretty much do.

The lieutenant prodded Pete to change into his pajamas, then supervised as Pete crossed the hall to the bathroom where Billy stood splashing toothpaste all over the mirror.

"Boy, are you in trouble," Billy gloated, cavity-fighting froth dribbling down his chin.

Pete ignored the taunt as he always did, this time with the added bonus of knowing he might be away from his horrid brother's harassment in a matter of hours. He took extra pleasure in flossing his teeth, a task he usually disdained. That night the waxy thread would be used like a James Bond gadget. The thought delighted Pete.

I need some sort of diversion to make sure Dad doesn't see me pocket the floss. Can't take any chances.

As Billy pushed by him to leave the bathroom, Pete shifted his weight and put his foot out just enough for Billy to trip over it and do a belly flop in the hallway. At the same time, Pete placed the tiny floss box in his pajama shirt pocket.

"Sorry, Billy," Pete said as he stepped over him to go back to his room, biting the inside of his lip to hide a smile.

Two for one. Floss & flop.

Talking over Billy's whining, Lt. Drake said, "This will all be over tomorrow, Junior. After your mother brings you lunch, we three Drake men will get out and break a sweat together raking leaves. Sound good?"

Pete suspected that was his father's best attempt at making amends.

"I asked you a question, Junior."

"Sounds great, Dad."

His father patted him on the back and closed the door, jiggling the knob.

Even though Pete intended to stay awake, he set the alarm on his clock radio for 4:30 a.m. and turned the volume to a level he hoped would be just loud enough to wake him without rousing anyone else. Now it was a matter of waiting.

Pete was seated in his desk chair willing the minutes to tick by when he heard the doorknob turn. Without sufficient time to dive into bed, he turned and pretended to make shadow puppets in front of the slits of light coming in the window from the streetlamps.

"Is that you, Dad? What are you doing up?"

Check-ups after lights-out were not something he had anticipated.

His father raised an eyebrow. "I could ask you the same."

"I wasn't sleepy."

"That's because you slept too much earlier. Now go on, get in bed, son."

Too risky. What if I really do fall asleep? Or Dad hears the letter rustle in the pillowcase?

"I'm pretty sick of lying in bed. Can't I just sit here awhile?"

His father cogitated briefly. "All right – but I expect you rested and energetic when we rake the leaves tomorrow."

"Yes, sir." Pete made a point to answer in a tone both respectful and obedient in hopes his father would be satisfied and leave the room before finding anything that would expose the top-secret plot.

The lieutenant walked to the window and pulled hard on a few of the boards, none of which budged. "Don't forget. I'm right down the hall." He exited the room, once again remanding Pete to the darkness.

Twenty minutes later, the light streaming in from under the doorway extinguished.

Pete nodded off in his chair numerous times, each time waking in greater panic that he'd overslept.

Finally, at 4:10 he chose to deactivate his alarm.

The time had come.

He stood in the center of his room for several moments, his mind a blank as to what his scheme entailed. Then it came flooding back.

First, he changed into street clothes, then put his pajamas on over them as camouflage in case his father walked in on him mid-breakout. Once dressed, he took the signed letter out of his pillowcase and folded it twice, trying to decide where to store it for safest keeping. He feared it might fall out of his pockets, so he tucked it inside one of his shoes and placed them by the door for easy last-minute retrieval.

Now it was time for the door doodad to be assembled. He tossed the bubble gum into his mouth and chewed furiously. Meanwhile, he tied the end of the dental floss to a paper clip and got up on his desk chair to push the clip through the space between the top of the door and the doorframe.

To his dismay, the clip was too short to go all the way through. He used another clip to push the first one along and lost it on the other side of the door in the process. He cringed as he listened for the sound of the falling object. Thankfully, the carpet muffled it.

The space between the top of the door and frame was much thinner than he anticipated, and he was at a loss as to how to push his implements of egress through the opening. Certainly, his ruler was too thick. A baseball card would work, but the lieutenant had impounded them all.

If only I had a piece of paper – that might do the trick.

There was only one sheet of paper left in his room, and thus, only one option.

He removed the academy letter from his shoe, and using one of the remaining paper clips, poked a tiny hole at the top of the page, just above the school logo. He then threaded the end of the dental floss through the hole and tied it tightly. Lt. Drake, being a Marine, had made a point to teach his sons proper knot tying.

Pete nearly fell when trying to climb back onto his chair in the room that was darker than he was used to. The only slivers of light came from the moon shining between the slats the lieutenant had used to cover the windows. As such, Pete's labor was slow going and the darkness disorienting.

Bit by bit, Pete fed the paper through the space above the door. Once the sheet was on the hall side of the door, he gradually let out the dental floss until he thought he felt a change in tension that he deduced meant the letter touched the ground. Clutching the container of floss as if it were a lifeline, he cautiously got down from the chair, letting the floss out little by little to compensate for his change in altitude.

He then prostrated himself to look under the door for signs of the paper. It was too dark to make out any shapes, so he felt on the floor against the wall for the ruler he'd placed there earlier in anticipation of using it to keep the door wedged open. Once he had the ruler in hand, he swept it under the door, trying to connect with the paper on the other side.

When the ruler made contact with the paper, he whisked the edge of the letter under the door toward him. Pinching a corner of the document, he pulled it into the room while simultaneously letting out more of the floss—praying the floss box contained enough twine to finish the task.

It did.

With the dental floss successfully wrapped vertically around the outside of the door, he could use the floss to hoist the TV cable. He ripped the floss tie off the letter, bent the long cable into a U, tied the floss securely to the U, and gave the knot a tug to ensure the floss wouldn't slip off the cable.

If anyone walks by now, hopefully they won't notice the strand of dental floss hanging from my door ... After all, it's white, and just a thin string and ... What am I doing wasting my time thinking about how dental floss looks?!

Okay, only two steps left.

He took the gum from his mouth and stuck it to the spot on the cable where the floss was attached. He then slid the cable loop under the door, gum-side-up. The cable rolled, causing both the gum and cable to stick to the carpet.

Uh oh.

He wiggled the cable until it dislodged from the carpet and again moved freely, but he couldn't tell what had become of the gum.

It's either stuck on the floor or still on the cable. Either way, I have to keep going.

Slowly pulling on the floss, he elevated the cable to the level where he estimated the doorknob was situated, then eased back on the floss, attempting to lower the cable loop over the knob. Floss in one hand, cable ends in the other, he gently pulled on the cable, hoping to feel resistance that would suggest the cable was hanging over the knob. This task proved more difficult than he'd expected. His hands went sweaty, his grip slippery.

When at last he pulled back on the cable ends and the cable didn't move, he felt certain the cable was looped over the doorknob. Just then, the floss fumbled out of his clammy grasp.

Oh nooooooo! I'm sunk!

I failed. My plan failed!

What am I gonna ...

... Wait a minute ... The cable's already looped over the doorknob. I don't need the floss anymore ... I think.

... No, I'm sure!

He exhaled slowly.

Time for the final maneuver.

Now with both hands free, he took one end of the cable in each hand, and keeping the tension taut, he steadily pulled one side of the cable then the other to turn the knob until he both heard and felt an indistinct click.

After drying his free hand on his pajamas, he turned the knob and opened the door a crack.

A stadium crowd cheered in his head.

Emboldened, he stretched his arm to feel around the floor for the ruler again, then wedged it between the door and the side of the frame to ensure the door could not fully close. At last, he loosened his grasp on the cable and stood, reaching his hand around the door to turn the locking button on the knob to an unlocked position, then removed the cable, floss, and gum. Remnants of the gum remained on the knob, but total cleanup would have to wait. Being reprimanded for a sticky doorknob would be the least of his worries next time he saw his father.

Pushing the door nearly shut again, he let the ruler do its job of keeping the door ajar while he tended to his last-minute preparations. Even though he'd unlocked the door, he was taking no chances when it came to getting locked back in.

No way do I want to go through that cable ordeal again!

He then threw off his pajamas, put on his shoes, and positioned his pillows and bedding to make it look like he was under the covers.

It was time to go.

His breathing shallow, he placed his hand on the knob, pausing to weigh his decision. There would be no undoing what he was about to do. And there was no guarantee his father would let him back in the house if he walked out the front door.

The thought of the last hug he received from his mother flashed in his mind, along with the strange words she'd said. She was the most important person in his life, and if his going away could somehow help her—whether by improving her health so she could cut back on her soul-sucking medication or by taking some of the strain off his parents' relationship—it was well worth the risks, whatever they may be.

He cracked the door open and had just lifted his foot to take a step when he was overcome by a wave of anxiety.

Something's wrong.

CHAPTER THIRTEEN – AWAITING THE DAWN

{Kapta Ánenn-Fui}

Pete was certain he heard his father's footsteps approaching, until he realized the sound was only the pounding of his own heart. Still, he was overcome with the feeling something about his plan was off.

I have no idea what it could be. It all worked. And I know Mom signed the letter.

He felt inside his shoe to make sure the Omni letter was safe, and all but came unglued when he failed to find it. It was then he remembered he'd left it on the floor. He dropped to his knees, scurrying around in the darkness to search for it. He knocked his head on both the bedframe and a desk leg before his hand landed on the paper. Hastily folding the parchment, he stuffed it back in his shoe and double-knotted the laces for added security.

My nerves can't take much more.

After poking his head into the black hallway and hearing nothing, he stepped out and closed the door behind him, then held his breath and tiptoed down the hall. Making his way through the living room, his feet labored to move across the carpet, as if he was having one of those dreams where you can't seem to get anywhere. The quiet was so pronounced it nearly hurt.

He strained to listen for the inevitable click of a lamp switch that would signal capture by his father who undoubtedly was sitting in his armchair in the dark, ready to pounce. No such click occurred.

The streetlamps on the lane cast eerie shadows, and through the living room window, Pete thought he saw a human shape duck behind the tree in the front yard. He watched his trembling hand reach for the knob on the front door, even as he waited for the expected feel of a palm clamping down on his shoulder. Opening the front door without incident, he dared a look back into the room. He was alone, and he was leaving.

So far, so miraculously good.

... Maybe too good.

He was tempted to peer behind the tree in the yard, but if there was indeed someone there, he had no interest in encountering them, especially since doing so could result in a situation that would awaken his father. Instead, he stole down the walkway and gingerly jogged across the row of front lawns, using the grass to quiet his steps. After rounding the first corner, he picked up speed and soon was sprinting toward the park, excitement propelling him.

Five minutes into his jog, he pulled up short, a bucket full of ice-cold practicality pouring into his brain and freezing him to the spot.

What am I doing?! I can't just take off and go to some weird new school in a place I know nothing about!

He turned back toward home, kicking himself for his momentary lapse in judgment.

Maybe I can pretend I was sleepwalking ... or that the academy people abducted me, but I got away and came home by choice.

He stood on one foot to take the acceptance letter from his sneaker. The tail end of his mother's signature was smudged by a teardrop. She'd taken a tremendous risk by signing the letter, given Lt. Drake's adamant stand against Pete going to the academy. He read the letter over and over, paying no attention to the words.

Eventually, he folded the letter and returned it to his shoe. Slowly, he pivoted, nearly buckling under the weight of his assorted worries. Then once again he took off for the park.

The night was moonless, but he had no trouble navigating his way. By the time he made it to the park's willow tree, he was wheezing hard. He'd never defied his father before, never done anything controversial or risky before.

Come to think of it, I've never really done much of anything before.

Collapsing onto the cool grass, he sat with his back against the tree as he'd done when talking to Leon less than a day prior. Only a few days back he'd been in his old house, packing, cursing the red X on his calendar, and scoffing when his mother suggested the new town may pose a grand adventure. Never in his wildest imaginings would he have guessed he'd be where he was at that moment, waiting in a deserted park for strangers to spirit him off to another dimension.

He stuck a finger inside his shoe to make sure the letter was still safe. The crepe texture against his finger placated him, and his breath came easier with each moment—though he still worried his father might somehow nab him.

Night yielded to morning as the warming rays of a new day yawned over the horizon. The denizens of the park rustled through the foliage, the early birds fluttered their wings and hunted worms, and all of nature came gradually to life.

"Bear claw?" called a cheerful voice.

"Huh?" Pete turned to see Etta approaching, holding before her a bag of breakfast pastries. "Oh, no, thanks. I'm too nervous to eat."

"Nothing to be nervous about as long as you have your acceptance letter. You do have it, don't you?"

He nodded.

"And it's signed?"

He nodded again.

"Not by you, correct?"

"Not by me."

"Good. You have any trouble getting out of the house?"

"It was pretty much just a matter of making pigs fly."

Drawing close, she stopped and cocked her head to evaluate his drab beige ensemble. "Is that what you're wearing to your first day at the Ocademy? You know what they say about making a first impression."

"All my clothes are like this."

"Not for long. Ah, here comes Leon now. Felilum, Leon!"

"He be havin' the letter?"

"He be … He does."

"And be it signed?"

Pete reached into his shoe and extracted the sweat-soaked document, handing it to Etta.

She scrunched up her face as she grasped the soggy paper with the tips of her fingers, holding it at arm's length until Leon was close enough to take it from her.

Leon unfolded it then held a large clear proboscis gadget over his nose. Bringing the paper to his face, he inhaled deeply. The false nose filled with rainbow fog. "Smells like everythin' be in order," he burbled, removing the snout and shaking Pete's hand. "Congratula-shi-ons, son. You be goin' to t'Academy of Omniosophical Arts and Sciences."

Etta cheered.

"Great!" Pete said. After a few awkward seconds of silence, he added, "Umm, how do we get there?"

Leon chuckled and turned to Etta. "I done keep forgettin' he not be knowin'."

Etta chuckled in turn. "Me too! Peyton, since we're here on so-called *Earth*, we do it the earth way."

"Uh, what way is that?"

"He's just a babe in the Arbin woods, isn't he?" she remarked to Leon.

Pete wondered if the two would continue talking about him in the third person.

"Here be how it works, son. When you done get to t'Ocademy, you'll done be placed in your natural element – after the Appraisement whirlwind, that be. They'll be goin' over all of that during o-rien-ta-shi-on."

"They sure will," Etta concurred with a giggle. "I envy you. You're going to love Ignis."

"What's that? Some sort of food?"

Etta laughed so hard she couldn't speak. Leon patted her back to help her catch her breath.

As the sun rose, so did Pete's apprehension over the odds his father might collar him before he could transport.

"Please, just tell me what to do and I'll do it."

The Custodian and Guardener exchanged an amused glance.

Etta shrugged. "All right then, suit yourself. Now remember, what works here with earth won't work with air or water or fire or wood."

"Okay?"

"Or metal," Leon added. "Can't be overlooking them."

"Very true. Thank you for the reminder, Leon. Platen deserves better than to be an afterthought. Now, Peyton, you see that gopher hole there at the base of the tree?"

"Yeahhhh?" he drawled tentatively.

"Go ahead and put your hand in – all the way up to the elbow."

"Wait! Do what?!" He considered the alternative of going home and back to bed. "I mean, won't some gopher bite my hand and give me rabies or something?"

"Hardly … well, at least not likely." Etta giggled again. "Simply plunge your arm in and someone on the other side will pull you through."

"On the other side of what?!" Pete warbled.

"On t'other side o' the portal – at t'Ocademy."

"I don't get it."

"Once you be cleared to transport on your own, you won't be needin' assistance, but all new recruits be getting' a helping hand, so to be speakin'."

The explanation made sense, as much sense as anything about the absurd situation could make.

"And you guys will follow right behind me?"

"Us? Snakes alive, noooooooo," Etta said.

Leon put his arm around Etta's shoulder. "Our place be here. Carin' for those who be stayin' behind."

"Where would the region be without its Custodian or Guardener?" Etta posited.

Leon wiggled all over. "*Euff*, I done shudder to think on't."

Etta pointed to the ascending sun.

"Scabs! Looks like we be out of time. Good luck, young Drake." Leon put one hand over his heart and the other to his lips. "Cheriste som."

Etta echoed the gesture and phrase.

"That's just what my mom said!"

"Of course it is, dear." Etta shooed Pete toward the small mound of dirt. "Now put your hand in the hole."

He pushed up his sleeve and bent down, reaching toward the hole.

Maybe if I put my hand in really fast nothing will be able to bite my fingers off.

"Wait!" Leon shouted.

"Aaaagh!" Pete screamed, jumping back in expectation of a vicious varmint blasting out of the hole to attack him.

"He'll not be gettin' far without this!" Leon hurriedly hobbled over to Pete, waving the crucial document that was still in his hand.

"Whew, that was close," Etta said. "Go on now. Scat!"

Pete grabbed the recruitment letter, closed his eyes, and thrust his arm down the hole. The tight clamping sensation on his flesh let him know there was indeed something there, and it had him firmly in its grasp.

Then it pulled—hard—and the portal closed behind him.

THE END

of life as Pete knew it

NOMINALLY ENTERTAINING GLOSSARY

of terms that may be foreign to you depending on your species and dimension of residence—some terminology will become clearer as you read subsequent story installments

LEGEND:

** Naturim language word(s) spelled phonetically in the modern People's Parlance. (You'll learn more about this in the next book)*

" Quoted phrase

Academy of Omniosophical Arts & Sciences – The Omniverse's pre-eminent institution of interdimensional tutelage and advancement since ante-antiquity.

Alarm – A torture device created to obliterate pleasant somnambulant wanderings and cause one to face the day in a state of abject panic and despair.

Arbin* – Of or relating to Arbis, the wood element and one of the academy domains.

Artichoke – This robust purple and green flower is a favorite among Terrin (earth element) brides who traditionally bite off the sharp tips of their bouquet's florets after reciting their nuptial vows. The prevalence of bridal choking led to the *artichoke* designation of these flowers originally named *kaktos*. In Dimension Q (where you most likely live), chokes are most frequently grown in the classical realms as well as the mythic oasis known as California.

Auto-Scrub – Automatic vehicle-washing device in the inventing stage, as conceived and designed by Peyton Drake.

Avocado – This large single-seeded berry, sometimes called *the alligator pear* owing to its bumpy tough-skinned exterior, boasts sedative as well as aphrodisiac qualities. The denizens of California are reputed to be addicted to the rich, creamy fruit, including it in nearly every food dish they serve.

Bacon – Made from the cured skin of the rare Porcine Pomelo, this member of the citrus family is a favorite among Dimension Q inhabitants, especially males from Gaia who possess excessive amounts of testosterone.

Ballerina – A ballet dancer. Ballet is an acutely formalized type of dance created in Dimension T as a form of punishment. Practitioners of the art (almost always those incarcerated for physical violence) are made to don unnatural footwear known as *pointe shoes* (the word *pointe* refers to the penal system making a *point* to discipline inmates) while attempting to move gracefully, showing no signs of the agony their feet are suffering.

Barmpot – Pejorative Northern English term for an objectionable and foolish person.

Baseball cards – A bygone form of idolatry and capitalistic commerce whereby images of athletes were printed on small pocket-sized cards. Consumers were encouraged to either keep, sell, or trade the cards as a means of earning extra cash and boasting rights. (If the braggart collector's own face was on the cards, that would be something to be proud of.)

Battle – Planned and strategized combat between warring factions. A portion of a greater (greater in terms of quantity, not quality) war.

Bed – A concept devised by the Aethereans (aether element), bed is a personal refuge of supreme comfort and rest. Many of life's most enjoyable and memorable activities take place *in bed.* Accessories known as *pillows* make the bed experience nothing short of rapturous.

Blanket fort – A place of refuge for those seeking solace in a suburban home. A stronghold constructed of cozy bedding.

Bone-colored – The age-old tradition of decorating one's habitat with the bones of their conquered foes has given way to more genteel forms of customization, i.e. paint that resembles the color of human bones. Paint cans should be kept away from young children who are known to drink the paint, believing it to be bone marrow soup. This can be a costly, messy, and poisonous mistake.

Box – A usually rectangular cardboard container that is a favorite object of play and diversion among cats, i.e. the species that rules Gaia (what Dimension Q denizens know as Earth).

Brisk – *Punctually, on the dot* as pertains to the measurement of time.

Bubble gum – Created to strengthen the jaws of carnivorous warriors in Dimension Omicron, the inadvertent *treat* became wildly popular in the Age of Nostalgia. That is, until sentients began losing all their teeth.

Butter Rum Lifesavers – Thumbnail-sized rings of hard candy that when sucked on can take away the woes of the day, thus making them worthy of their boastful moniker.

By the: bayou, binary, byway" – Colloquial forms of segue used in conversational speech.

Cake – A soft sweet food baked into a pan or mold and served at times of celebration—every day being an opportunity for celebration; the means of appeasing malcontent fae. Prudent denizens of Terris keep cake on hand at all times, just in case.

Car – Originally short for *carriage*, it is a road vehicle comprised of four wheels, an internal combustion engine, and (most important) a radio. The superior forms of automobiles have a retractable roof allowing drivers to enjoy the elements as well as attention from the opposite sex.

Carmen Miranda – Born Maria do Carmen Miranda da Cunha, *The Brazilian Bombshell* was a samba singer popular for her fruit-laden apparel. While observers assumed the fruit represented a fashion statement, in truth, Miss Miranda often became peckish while shooting films in Hollywood. The fruits provided a quick fix, enabling her to continue to work without her stomach growling.

Carpe diem" – A rallying cry coined by Horace, the literal meaning is *seize the day*; not to be confused with the Aquin (water element) term *carperdiem* indicating a daily allowance of fish.

Carrot – A vegetable enjoyed both cooked and raw, the latter, especially with *dip*. The term for something used as an incentive.

Casserole – A one-dish meal that starts off with the humblest and often most disparate of ingredients. Thanks to the magical powers inherent to the modern-day oven, the dish miraculously transforms into something palatable, if not delicious. Curiously, many of these hodge-podge concoctions taste better the next day, especially cold!

Cassette player – A palm-sized plastic compact through which a ribbon of tape is run, resulting in the playing of glorious music; a wily invention prone to get stuck beneath a car seat or gas pedal.

Catapult – A delightful device whereby tension is harnessed and suddenly released to hurl an object or (preferably) a person. Fun for the whole family.

Cheriste som*" – Generally used as a sign-off to a conversation, the Naturim phrase translates to: *Above all, love.*

Chocolate – An edible substance made from sweetened ground cacao seeds. A form of currency in certain realms, an irresistible aphrodisiac in others. Its magical properties have been known to quell the ire of shrews and harpies.

Cigar box – While the smoking of cigars is taboo for young boys in most dimensions, the boxes themselves have long been the preferred form of treasure storage for Dimension Q lads. Expect to find *baseball cards*, *marbles*, and *yo-yos* in these portable vaults.

Clusterfail" – A convoluted or messy situation involving multiple individuals or entities.

Cold as an Aurelean moon" – Referring to the coldest area in the Omniverse, the moons of Aurelea boast a temperature of -2.3 Kelvin. Thus, the term implies something is a bit chilly.

Cordless drill – Part of the grouping called *power tools*, the automated drilling device obviates the necessity of manual labor. Despite the fact such automation serves to weaken the arm power of the user, males in possession of power tools feel a marked increase in virility and self-worth.

Custodian – Steward who watches over and protects the dimensional denizens of an assigned region. Custodians work closely with their local Guardeners.

Defensive tackle – In the curiously named Gaia sport of football, this term refers to a player whose job it is to clog the middle of the defensive line so as not to allow members of the offensive team to get by them, thereby depriving the offense of the opportunity to gain ground and/or score.

Dental floss – An oral hygiene product used in dimensions where beings possess teeth. Generally put to use by those who do not possess hair strands long enough or strong enough to do the job.

Deora – The generic term for all that is good and wonderful in the Omniverse; the Omniverse itself; the all-in-all, the great creatrix. Often used in explanatory phrases such as: *For Deora's sake, Deora forbid, Exalted Deora!*

Dim – The common term used to refer to a dimension, meaning one of the infinite realms that make up the omniversal space-time-dimension continuum; not to be construed as a slur regarding a lack of intelligence.

Dim Phi fiddle – The phrase *fit as a Dim Phi fiddle* refers to Dimension Phi and means *ready for use, in good shape*.

Diner – An eating establishment often constructed from (or made to look like) a train dining car; often open 'round the clock; patrons expect swill-like coffee, greasy grilled fare, and friendly service by a waitress with a heart of gold and a storied past.

Dinner – The heaviest meal of the day, served midday in manual labor communities, served after work for those engaged in non-physical labor.

Doodad – A whimsical contrivance created to perform a simple task using complicated steps; as much a form of entertainment as it is a machine of function. The term was coined by Peyton Drake of Dimension Q.

Doohickey – Drake's original name for the Doodad.

Draft – Compulsory recruitment; the early stage of a writing project when the work is rubbish; a sneaky bit of wind that enters a structure uninvited.

Dragon – The term for a winged fire-breathing reptile, usually six feet in height and 30 feet in length with a wingspan of 60-90 feet. Just as caterpillars in the majority of realms go through a pulverizing metamorphosis when transforming into butterflies, dragons often start off as serpents. Warm-weather dragons (nearly 75%) are born via egg. The remaining 25% that inhabit colder climes are born ovoviviparously, fully formed from their parent's womb, since the ground is too cold to allow for proper incubation. Egg-laying dragons may produce as many as 100 eggs in a litter, but only 1-5 of the eggs usually turn into dragons. This is not because the other eggs perish. They are lain as a means of subterfuge to confuse and mislead would-be predators. The species is thought to be extinct in Dimension Q.

Duct tape – Invented in 1942 and originally named *duct tape* because of its ability to slough off water, this versatile Dimension Q adhesive was initially used to keep ammunition casings waterproof. In 1945 the product became the go-to adhesive for holding ventilation ducts together, and henceforth was referred to as *duct* tape. Quickly, it became apparent that the product was good for nearly every sort of repair, going so far as mending broken marriages.

Earthquake – Similar to how a person will shudder or thrash about when being vexed by an insistent insect, the surface of the earth tremors when something is *bugging* it. If Earth is tickled, its quaking is accompanied by a rumbling laugh.

Edisyuh id Deora*" – A cry for immediate assistance, translated from Naturim (the first language) as: *Help me, creatrix.*

Element – A particular or fundamental aspect of something, especially one that is vital, primary, or characteristic; that which relates to or embodies the essence and powers of the natural world.

Estate – Sometimes used to suggest a vast expanse of personally owned land on which sits a grand abode, thereby conveying a sense of wealth. At the academy, the term refers to the element domain in which a student lives.

Father – A figure (often male) who serves as protector and provider for those in his/her/its/hemm care. A generic term for a male who provides seed required for propagation. Someone credited with the origination or early history of an ideology, fad, or new *thing*.

Felilum* – A salutation. *Good day/morning.*

Fly fisherman – In Dimension Q a fly fisherman refers to an angler who employs an artificial fly as a lure to catch fish, using various methods of casting a line across the water (as opposed to casting a line down into it) from a fishing pole. Occasionally, when a lake is especially still, you can hear tiny screams of agony from the supposedly *artificial* flies. In other dimensions, fly fishing refers to the fae activity of capturing horse flies with the intention of riding them. Horse fly rodeos are a popular draw in many realms. The blood-sucking female horseflies are known to put up quite a fight.

Football – Many believe this gridiron sport was created by someone who was either drunk or lost a dare, as the game has nothing to do with *feet.* The *ball* in question is pointed at two ends and doesn't do the rolly thing one expects a ball to do. Though technically the purpose of the game is to score goals, the bulk of activity involves tackling opponents and slamming them to the ground in heaps.

For cryin' out loud" – A Dimension Q minced oath euphemism expressing surprise or displeasure.

Gaia – If you are reading this, you are here. The third planet from a star called Sol, located in the Aakash Ganga (a.k.a. the Milky Way), Local Group, Virgo Supercluster, Laniakea; often mis-referenced as Earth.

Gold Volcano – A trophy bestowed in Dimension Q to a young inventor for excellence in design and functionality; a highly coveted honor.

Goldilocks – A fairy tale about a blonde girl who breaks into the home of a bear family, messes up their beds, busts one of their chairs, and eats their food, all the while complaining about the quality of their home furnishings and hospitality.

Good Gobfinkle!" – A popular exclamatory phrase indicating shock or surprise. Gobfinkle was a newscaster known for his shocking headline announcements as well as his practice of dressing in a way that camouflaged him with the environment so he could jump out of his surroundings to surprise bystanders on camera.

Gopher – A burrowing rodent skilled in digging tunnels; also a person who is sent on miscellaneous, menial errands.

Green army men – Two-inch tall molded plastic toy soldiers, generally olive green in color, often standing on a solid plastic base to keep them upright, nearly always wielding a weapon of some sort, usually from the 20th century. The low cost of the items made them a favorite of Peyton Drake who tended to destroy the little soldiers when trying out his latest warfare gadgetry.

Guardener – Academy sentinel charged with deciding who is admitted into the dimension to be guarded; works closely with the local Custodian.

Hi" – Pronounced *hai*, it is a Dimension Q, Gaia greeting, now part of the People's Parlance (what you may know as English).

High school – A social battleground for teens in a majority of the dimensions. Under the guise of *education*, students face a litany of heinous life challenges including dealing with unsightly erupting facial pustules, extreme and usually unwarranted peer censure, issues of identity, the protocols of courting, and most egregious of all—parents! The term *high school* comes from the student tendency to get *high* on a myriad of narcotic substances designed to create artificial short-term euphoria.

Hula – A Polynesian dance usually associated with the idyllic Hawaiian Islands. Traditionally accompanied by oli (chant) or mele (song), it is comprised of six basic steps and is employed as a means of storytelling. In modern times in the West, the dance form is called auana (which means *to wander*) and is danced to music played by guitar, double bass, and most notably ukelele. The clothing most often associated with hula is a skirt made of long strands of grass and a brassiere made of halved coconut shells.

Jawing – Talking at length, chitchatting. This term has replaced the phrase *shooting the breeze* which was outlawed as cruel and inappropriate in Nitris (air element) realms.

Jot – A teeny tiny bit, the term was inspired by the name of the smallest letter in the Greek alphabet; brother of Iota.

Jugular – The neck or throat and its primary vein; a delicacy for bloodsucking newts and vampires.

Kale – A headless wild cabbage devoid of redeeming qualities. The drab vegetable rose to 21st century prominence when information on it was *tweeted* by a publicist whose *autocorrect* software mistakenly replaced the word *Kardashian* with *kale.* Both the K vegetable and K persons are similar in vacuous, faddish nature.

Kiss – Contact, generally made by human lips, on the flesh of another being. The touch is meant to convey affection, friendship, desire (that's a whole other level of kissing), or is used in greeting. It can also refer to a small bit of something such as a chocolate candy or sprinkling of perfume or sugar.

L'enfant terrible – A troublemaker; indiscreet, irresponsible instigator.

Laundry list – It remains to be satisfactorily explained why dirty clothes would request or require a list.

Leash – A tether generally used to restrain and guide a domesticated canine or the submissive in a domination relationship. The leash is usually clipped to a collar, a circle of metal or fabric that surrounds the neck.

Lieutenant – A junior commissioned officer in the armed forces, fire brigade, or constabulary. The rank may have subdivisions such as Lieutenant Commander, Second Lieutenant, Sub-lieutenant, Lieutenant Junior Grade. In the case of Lt. Drake whose commission is part of the U.S. Navy, the Army equivalent would be Captain, and Air Force equivalent Flight Lieutenant. Lt. Drake's insignia is comprised of two medium gold braid stripes. He's very proud of his stripes.

Lilliputian – Very small, a term coined by travel writer Jonathan Swift during his sojourn in the country of Lilliput, located in Dimension Tao.

Little Bo-Peep – In Pete's realm, the term refers to a nursery rhyme about a neglectful shepherdess accused of losing several of her sheep. In more advanced dimensions it is mentioned she loses her sheep when focused on a device called an iPhone. She is generally depicted in Lolita fashions; that is to say, wearing a short pastel capped-sleeve dress, white bloomers and stockings, and a bonnet. In addition to her mobile telephone, she carries a crook.

Little brother – A fraternal source of unending annoyance for most older siblings. Term used for anything that tests the boundaries of patience.

Long night – Colloquial phrase meaning comatose state.

Lunch – A midday meal in Dimension Q, less substantial than Splitz and often devoid of nutrients; a form of socialization observed by wealthy jobless spouses who have no purpose other than to criticize their friends and peers.

Marble – A small ball of swirled-colored glass used by adolescents (primarily males) in games and as currency. Units of knowledge contained in the cranium of certain species.

Marines – Formally known as the United States Marine Corps, this *power projecting* branch of the armed forces is especially formidable because of its ability to multitask on land, sea, and air. The original Marines (a strictly aquatic corps) merged with infantry units to defend naval vessels in 1775 A.D. The rest is modern history as well as a source of pride. The first troops chose the English Bulldog as their mascot, owing to the breed's natural tenacity and love of playing with squeaky toys in kiddie pools.

Marshmallow – A squishy edible cube made of sugar and gelatin; one of the staple ingredients of a Dimension Q culinary phenomenon known as *s'mores*.

Mongoose – A long, but small, feliform carnivorous mammal, venerated for its ability to handle venomous serpents. The term *silly* *mongoose* refers to a mongoose who shows off while serpent-taming and becomes distracted, thus being fatally bitten by the serpent.

Mother – In some species, a female child-bearer; a purveyor of warm fuzzy feelings and edible palliatives; the omniversal symbol of Deora's unqualified love.

Naturim – The primum lingua, language of the ancients. The Naturim phrases included herein are written using the People's Parlance alphabet. For pronunciation and syllabary, consult the *English~Naturim Lexicarta* available where Omni books are purveyed.

Ocademy" – An abbreviated term referring to the Academy of Omniosophical Arts & Sciences.

Okay" – A Dimension Q term phoneticized from the letters O and K. The debate over the term's origin has waged for fui anardsekk (three centuries). Some claim it comes from the phrase *oil correct* as in *all is correct* or even from the Greek *ochs* which was an incantation used to dispel fleas. Others attribute it to the 19th century Choctaw phrase *oke* meaning *it is* or the Wolof *waw- kay* indicating an emphatic *yes*. However, the French language seems to have the best claim to the term, either from the emphatic phrase *oh qu'oui* meaning *ah, yes* as noted in 1768, or the less likely term *aux quais* meaning *on the quays* as pertains to French sailors making appointments with American girls *on the quays* during the American Revolutionary War in the 1780s. The truth of the matter, though not chronicled, is the term comes from the marriage of Dimensions O and K that took place after their anil-long (of millennium duration) feud was resolved.

Omelette – An egg turnover whereby a disk of cooked egg is topped with appealing ingredients then folded over; a short prayer or mantra.

Omni – Translates as *all* or *of all things*, also used as an abbreviated name for the Academy of Omniosophical Arts & Sciences.

Omnigram – A written communique usually delivered by a Mercury Messenger travelling 750 miles per hour, just under the speed of sound so as not to create sonic thunder. (More on these delivery folk in future installments of Pete's story.)

Omniosophical – Related to the study of everything.

Omniverse – The Great All; the entirety of creation wherein the whole is infinitely more than the sum of its parts.

Over the moon" – Dimension Q phrase indicating joy and jubilance; the term was inspired by the event during which J.J. Flash leapt over the moon when his sweetheart, Jill, accepted his marriage proposal.

Pajamas – A fashion oxymoron insomuch as it is a seemingly formal buttoned-up jacket and pants ensemble designed for sleep and lounging.

Park – A rural pocket of an urban area; the source of life for cities; also a practice whereby hormonal teens stop their vehicles at a picturesque vista for the purpose of snogging.

People's Parlance – The modern omniversal language, currently what Gaia inhabitants know as English.

Pill – A small round or oval mass of curative meant to be ingested whole. Whether taken in medicated or placebo form, the expectation of relief on the part of the user often results in immediate change for the better.

Pillow – One of the most beloved personal comfort items in the Omniverse, this sewn bag of fluff, preferably filled with donated caladrius (healing bird) feathers, is a source of sublime rest and bliss. Used in tandem with a *bed*, it takes slumber to sublime heights.

Pizza – An Italian dish considered by many to be of divine origin, its ingredients are simple and irresistible when combined: a baked disk of dough covered in pulverized tomato secretions and moldy bovine lactation curds, often topped with meats or vegetables to glorious effect.

Platen – The newest (and final) omniversally recognized element (metal).

Porch – A covered area along the edge or perimeter of a home; a place of refuge and tranquility much loved by those looking to enjoy solace, sunsets, or sweet tea.

Portal – Transdimensional and interdimensional gateways.

Q-zer – A less than flattering term for a denizen of Dimension Q, often followed by the word *loser*.

Rabies – A viral mammalian disease transmitted via saliva; a fatal affliction that causes madness and convulsions prior to death.

Robe – A soft fluffy outer garment worn over pajamas when pajamas are deemed insufficient; a loose cloak or mantle.

Safety First – A moralistic Dimension Q science-themed comic book series for youths. Representative articles include the condescending *You May Not Be as Smart as You Think, and That's OK*; the sanctimonious *Don't Make Us Say We Told You So*; and the ignominious *Birds & Bees and Between the Knees*.

Salad – A mélange of things; also a cold dish comprised of a variety of vegetables, usually raw, and coated with a *dressing*. The term *salad days* refers to a time when one who is young or inexperienced. It derives from the idea that an inexperienced cook would be unable to properly prepare anything more complicated than a salad.

Scabs!" – An omniversal exclamation owing to the enjoyment produced by saying the word. It has no relation to the crusty substance that forms to protect an open wound during the healing process, nor does it refer to individuals who flout the dictates of the local union by showing up to work during a labor strike.

Scarabs!" – An Ignin (fire element) exclamation or invective indicating surprise.

Scrammer – Invention created by Peyton Drake at 6 years of age, designed to scramble eggs.

Silly mongoose" – Innocuous phrase used to gently tease someone when he/she/it/hemm says or does something absurd.

Slippers – Soft, comfortable, slip-on footwear meant to be worn indoors. Sometimes the bottoms are made of hard rubber or leather so that the slippers can be worn outside. This effectively defeats the idea of having slippers in the first place, not to mention it takes away their ability to slip.

Snake in the grass" – A sneaky individual who vows loyalty, but secretly betrays. This phrase is thought to have been coined by the Roman poet Virgil in 37 pre-R.C.

Snakes alive!" – Exclamatory phrase. Urban legend holds the saying came from a Gobi Desert dinner party gone wrong.

Sourmug – A scurrilous epithet for the noble and proud canine breed known as the Bulldog. The stocky animal walks with a pleasant rolling gait. Its body is compact, with a relatively large head, attractively folded ears, a suitably short muzzle, a lower jaw that protrudes somewhat. It wears an oversized fur suit resulting in wrinkles around the head and face. The breed is the equivalent of a clown baby or baby clown, depending on who you ask.

Stampede string – A length of twine attached to a hat and tightened under the chin to prevent the hat from flying off when the wearer is traveling at high speeds or stampeding through the streets of Pamplona.

Statue of Liberty – A transgender midsize neoclassical copper statue gifted by one principality to another on the planet Gaia. The initial reason for the gift concerned the accidental incineration of a group of nationals at a state dinner when the table-side torching of crème brûlée got out of hand.

Steel farthings – The basics, the essentials; similar to the Dimension Q phrase *brass tacks.*

Sticks in (one's) craw" – A phrase indicating a lingering bother or grievance.

Street clothes – Non-school-uniform apparel.

Sun – A fixed heavenly body of luminous gases held together by its own gravity, around which planets often orbit.

Swimming – Propulsion of the body through liquid—especially water—by use of the limbs, fins, or tail; a recreational activity in certain dimensions, a way of life in others.

Swing – A contraption and activity whereby a seat is hung from a girder and the one seated is pushed forth and back to engage the gravity stream, resulting in a physical effect of freedom that momentarily approximates flight; a type of dance whereby one of the partners is swung up into the air, over the shoulder, through the legs, up into the chandelier.

Television – A system of transmitting live or recorded action, images, and sound to a viewing screen; the means by which the Game of Thrones saga (sometimes referred to as The Great Betrayal) is witnessable in multiple dimensions.

Teppanyaki – Iron griddle Ignin (fire element) *quick-cooking*, often involving entertainment as chefs rapidly chop ingredients, create vegetable volcanoes, fling edibles into the mouths of delighted diners, and even juggle their cutlery.

Three Little Pigs (the) – A folktale about a trio of anthropomorphic swine who build their homes using disparate materials, each with differing degrees of success when it comes to preventing a noisome wolf from blowing their buildings down. Originally written in the med-aevum era as a holiday gimmick designed to sell bricks manufactured by the Folkestone Masonry Companye, the story caught on. In many dimensions, an animated film version of the tale is televised each sekkl around the time of the Autumnal Equinox harvest. Its viewing is a family tradition, usually featuring a feast with a pork roast as its centerpiece.

Thumb – A digit on the hand, separated from the array of fingers, and used for grabbing, as well as *hitchhiking* i.e. requesting complimentary transportation via use of the pollex. Despite the fact most thumbs are "opposable," they tend to get on together well.

Time trialist – An individual who races against the clock in his/her/its/hemm given sport. The competitor who travels the greatest distance in the shortest amount of time is crowned victor. One of the most fiercely contended trials is the Prologue stage of the annual cross-countries Tour de France, a duo-wheel race in Dimension Q that began in 1903 A.D. as a means of selling L'Auto newspapers.

Tire – A round, shock-absorbing wheel cover.

Toothbrush and toothpaste – Products used together to cleanse *teeth* i.e. small, bony enamel-covered body bits used by vertebrates to bite, tear, or chew. Since teeth collect debris, resulting in foul expulsions from the mouth, the “paste” is made of fresh-smelling ingredients meant to bathe and disinfect; the *brush* is used to spread the paste around and dislodge the wreckage lurking between the teeth.

Towel – Touted by Dim Zeta former Fiddlehead (and intergalactic hitchhiker) Douglas Noel Adams as the most indispensable item one can possess. In simplest terms, it is a length of absorbent cloth or paper used to dab or wipe surfaces and sentients dry. In reality, it is so much more.

Tree – A large-scale woody plant bearing branches, leaves, and sometimes fruit, nuts, or blossoms; ages-old planetary steward. In a host of dimensions, trees bring life to planets and shield the terrain from the relentless rays of a blazing sun.

VW Bug – The Volkswagen Käfer (People's car - beetle) was developed by Ferdinand Porsche in 1938 at the command of Dimension Q Gaia villain, Adolph Hitler. To this day, the Beetle line remains the longest-running, most manufactured automobile in Dimension Q Gaia history.

Waffle – A crisped, hand-sized butter cake made with the use of a patterned iron consisting of two hot metal plates, between which leavened batter is poured and cooked. The acclaimed waffle diner chain Jenny’s is owned by a drove of donkeys using the original recipe of matriarch Jenny Pace. Their catch phrase *hay is for horses* became overused by the same folk who insist on saying, “Well – that’s a very deep subject,” “Take a picture. It lasts longer,” and those who make rhymes employing the word *orange*. Jenny’s later changed their slogan to: *Every day’s a heyday at Jenny’s.*

War (Warfare) – Armed conflict between those who should know better, most often perpetrated by materialistic intergalactic bullies; outlawed in most dimensions.

Watch (noun) – Timepiece, chronometer, fashion accessory utilized to *watch* time; a manipulative device used to hypnotize humans who are obscenely susceptible to its powers and worship time nearly as much as they do currency. Time has become a trendy crutch and scapegoat in the younger dimensions.

Wazzak – A *crazy* person; used as a derogatory term.

When pigs fly" – A Gaia expression used to describe an impossible feat as (sadly) the swine on that particular planet are inexplicably incapable of flight, most likely owing to the atmosphere's gravity and the poor quality of porcine nutrition there.

Yahtzee – A dice game popular in Dimension Q's *wholesome family* era, the word is also used as an exclamatory cry of triumph.

Zombie – A member of the undead. A creature who becomes infected with the zombie virus loses all cognitive abilities as well as speech; however, they retain basic motor skills and get about on foot to feed on living flesh.

USE THE QR CODE BELOW

OR

TYPE IN THE TINY URL FOR THIS STORY'S LINK LIST

tinyurl.com/01MfA-Links

Acknowledgments

Thank you so much for teaming up with Pete as he begins his journey to the Ocademy. As you will find, Omni is about far more than a smattering of books. We are a collaborative community that focuses on immersive experiences and creative expression, all with a heart for philanthropy and service.

This series serves as the basis for our Reading Revolution program—a dynamic collection of parent workshops and interactive resources designed to win over reluctant readers and bring families together in meaningful, memorable ways.

This project wouldn't exist without the initial encouragement of Trish Miller and tireless editing efforts of Cindy Freeman.

To find out what's on the other side of the portal, continue on through the gopher hole to ***Destiny by Design***, Tomo 1, parsa ii of Pete's 49-novella saga

www.ingramcontent.com/pod-product-compliance
Lightning Source LLC
LaVergne TN
LVHW091008080826
845145LV00003B/1179

* 9 7 8 1 9 5 9 8 2 2 0 0 4 *